X
16

STONE ARCH BOOKS
a capstone imprint

STONE ARCH BOOKS™

Published in 2013
A Capstone Imprint
1710 Roe Crest Drive
North Mankato, MN 56003
www.capstonepub.com

Originally published by DC Comics in the U.S. in single magazine form as Batman Adventures #8.

DC Comics
1700 Broadway, New York, NY 10019
A Warner Bros. Entertainment Company

Printed in China by Nordica.
0413/CA21300442
032013 007226NORDF13

Cataloging-in-Publication Data is available at the Library of Congress website:
ISBN: 978-1-4342-6036-9 (library binding)

Summary: Batman faces off against the Black Mask! Whose side will the deadly Phantasm take? Plus, in a brooding back-up story, Bruce reflects on the many masks he wears.

STONE ARCH BOOKS

Ashley C. Andersen Zantop *Publisher*
Michael Dahl *Editorial Director*
Donald Lemke & Sean Tulien *Editors*
Heather Kindseth *Creative Director*
Bob Lentz & Alison Thiele *Designers*
Kathy McColley *Production Specialist*

DC COMICS

Joan Hilty *Original U.S. Editor*
Harvey Richards *U.S. Assistant Editor*
Kelsey Shannon *Cover Artist*

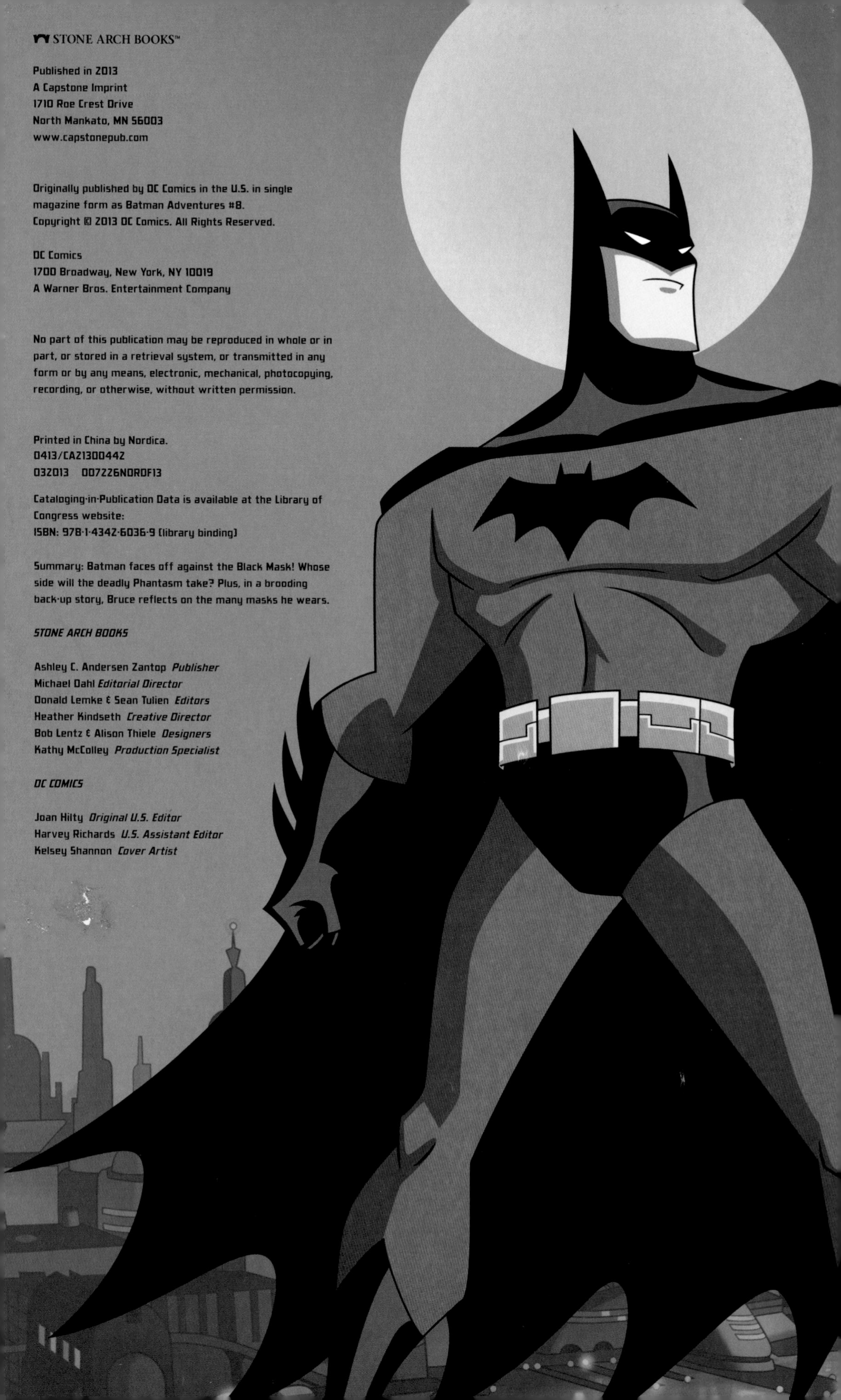

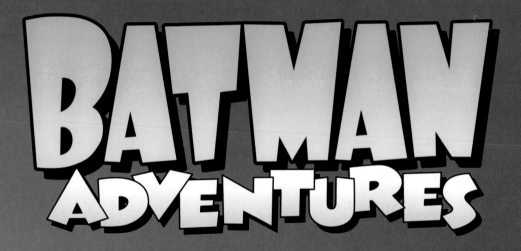

BATMAN ADVENTURES

MASQUERADE IN RED!

Dan Slott...writer
Rick Burchett ....penciller
Terry Beatty..inker
Lee Loughridge ....colorist
Jared K. Fletcher.......................................letterer

Batman created by
Bob Kane

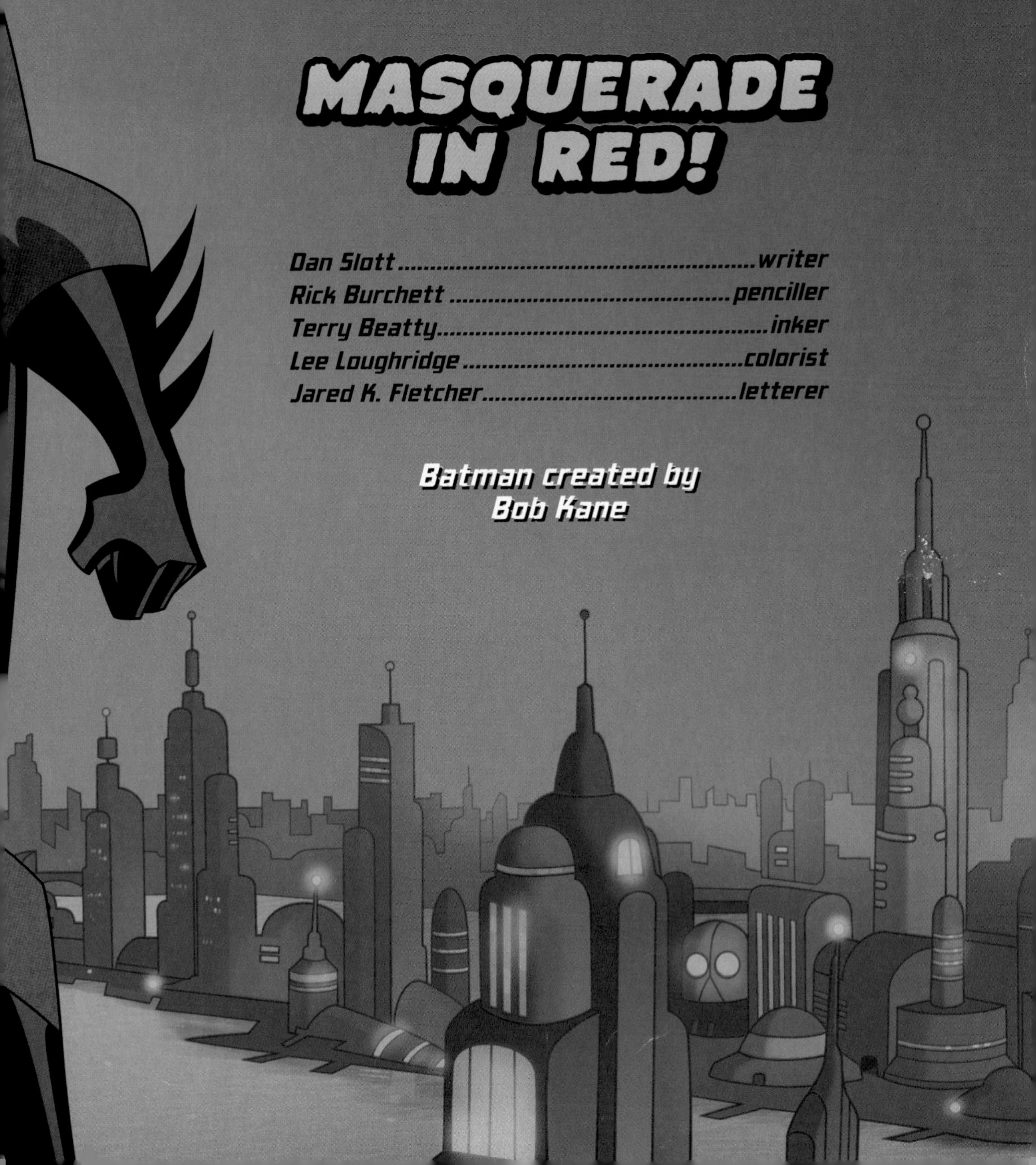

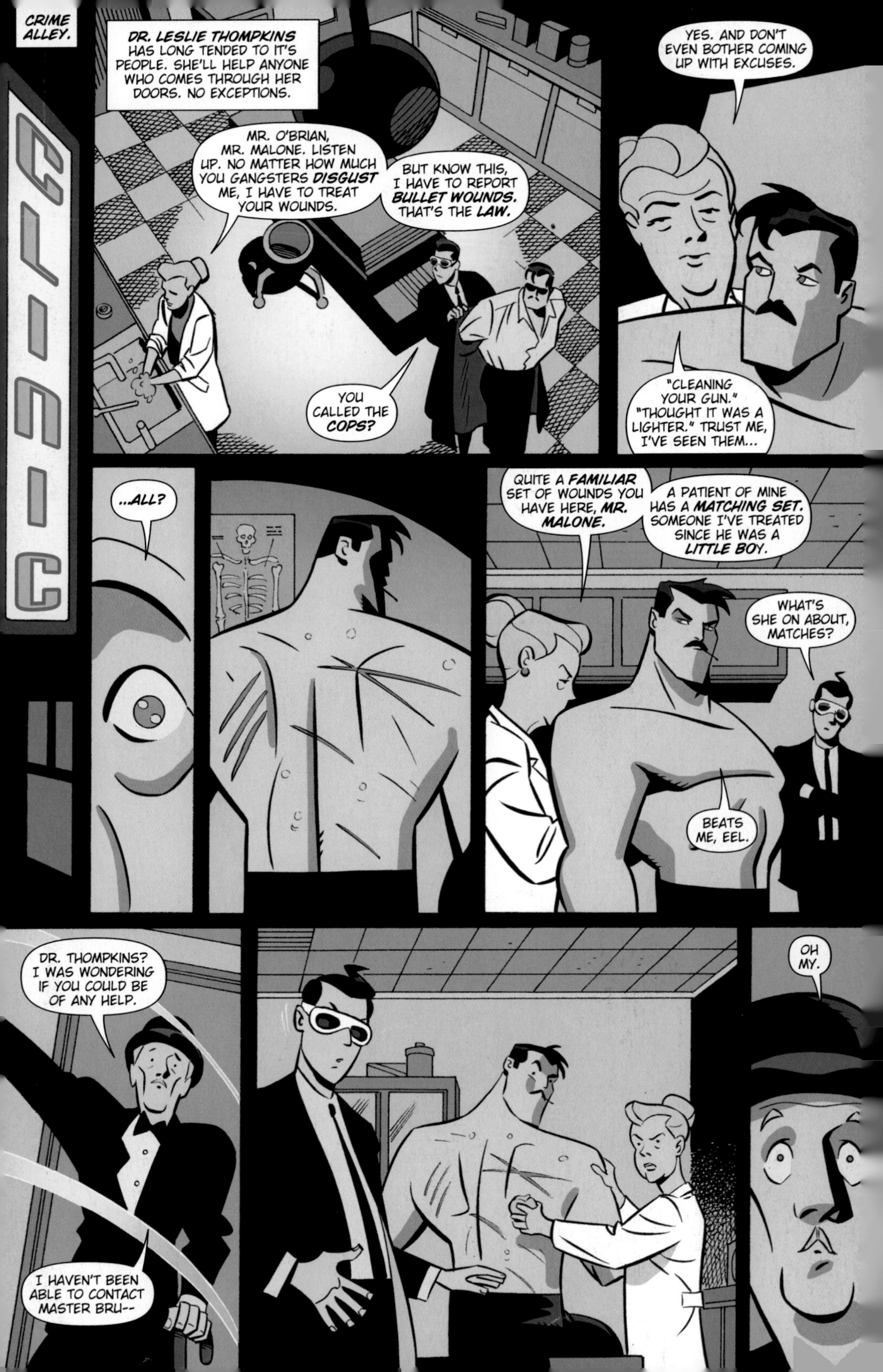

CRIME ALLEY.
CLINIC
DR. LESLIE THOMPKINS HAS LONG TENDED TO IT'S PEOPLE. SHE'LL HELP ANYONE WHO COMES THROUGH HER DOORS. NO EXCEPTIONS.
MR. O'BRIAN, MR. MALONE. LISTEN UP. NO MATTER HOW MUCH YOU GANGSTERS DISGUST ME, I HAVE TO TREAT YOUR WOUNDS.
BUT KNOW THIS, I HAVE TO REPORT BULLET WOUNDS. THAT'S THE LAW.
YOU CALLED THE COPS?
YES. AND DON'T EVEN BOTHER COMING UP WITH EXCUSES.
"CLEANING YOUR GUN." "THOUGHT IT WAS A LIGHTER." TRUST ME, I'VE SEEN THEM...
...ALL?
QUITE A FAMILIAR SET OF WOUNDS YOU HAVE HERE, MR. MALONE.
A PATIENT OF MINE HAS A MATCHING SET. SOMEONE I'VE TREATED SINCE HE WAS A LITTLE BOY.
WHAT'S SHE ON ABOUT, MATCHES?
BEATS ME, EEL.
DR. THOMPKINS? I WAS WONDERING IF YOU COULD BE OF ANY HELP.
I HAVEN'T BEEN ABLE TO CONTACT MASTER BRU--
OH MY.

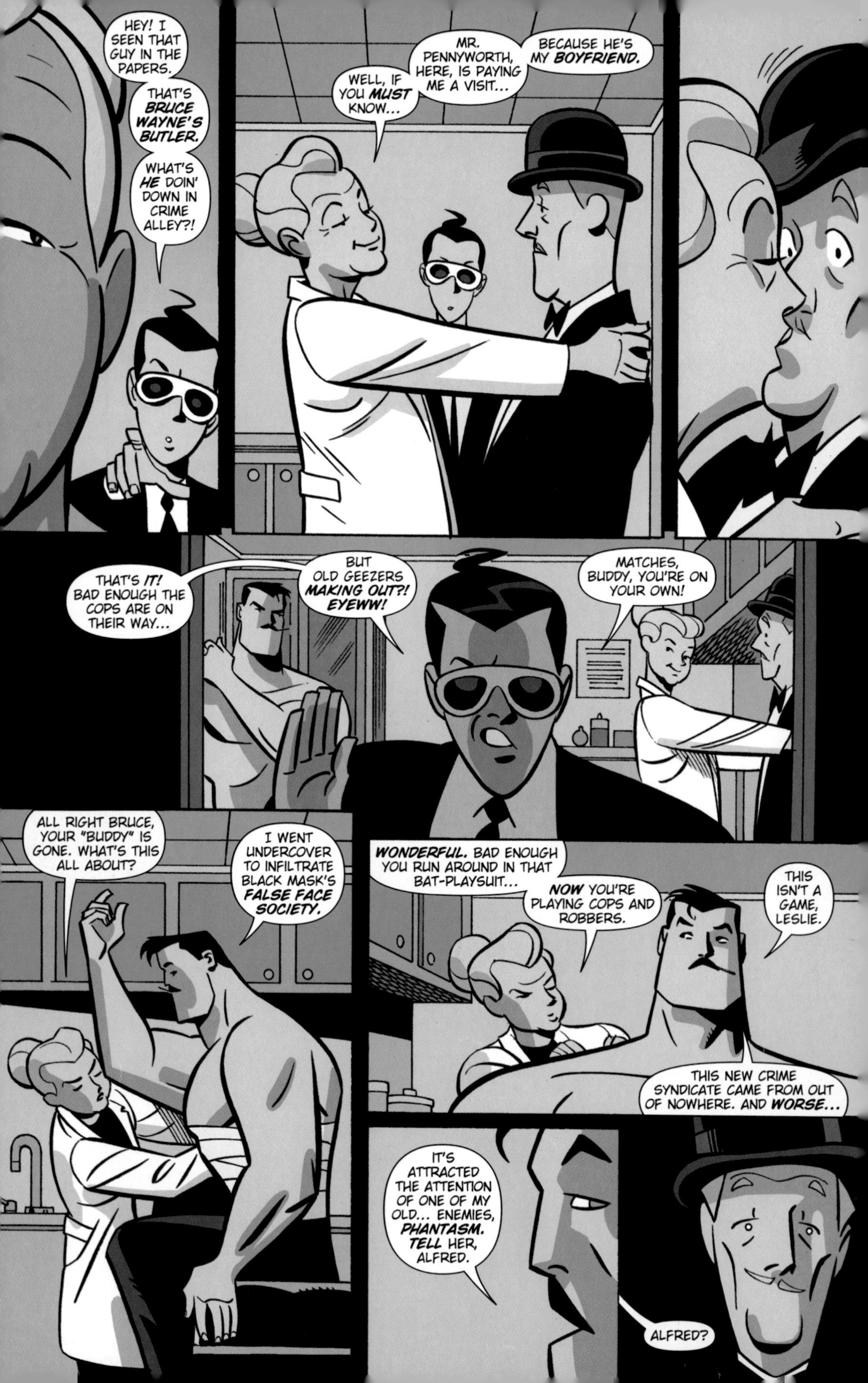
HEY! I SEEN THAT GUY IN THE PAPERS.
THAT'S BRUCE WAYNE'S BUTLER.
WHAT'S HE DOIN' DOWN IN CRIME ALLEY?!
WELL, IF YOU MUST KNOW...
MR. PENNYWORTH, HERE, IS PAYING ME A VISIT...
BECAUSE HE'S MY BOYFRIEND.
THAT'S IT! BAD ENOUGH THE COPS ARE ON THEIR WAY...
BUT OLD GEEZERS MAKING OUT?! EYEWW!
MATCHES, BUDDY, YOU'RE ON YOUR OWN!
ALL RIGHT BRUCE, YOUR "BUDDY" IS GONE. WHAT'S THIS ALL ABOUT?
I WENT UNDERCOVER TO INFILTRATE BLACK MASK'S FALSE FACE SOCIETY.
WONDERFUL. BAD ENOUGH YOU RUN AROUND IN THAT BAT-PLAYSUIT...
NOW YOU'RE PLAYING COPS AND ROBBERS.
THIS ISN'T A GAME, LESLIE.
THIS NEW CRIME SYNDICATE CAME FROM OUT OF NOWHERE. AND WORSE...
IT'S ATTRACTED THE ATTENTION OF ONE OF MY OLD... ENEMIES, PHANTASM. TELL HER, ALFRED.
ALFRED?

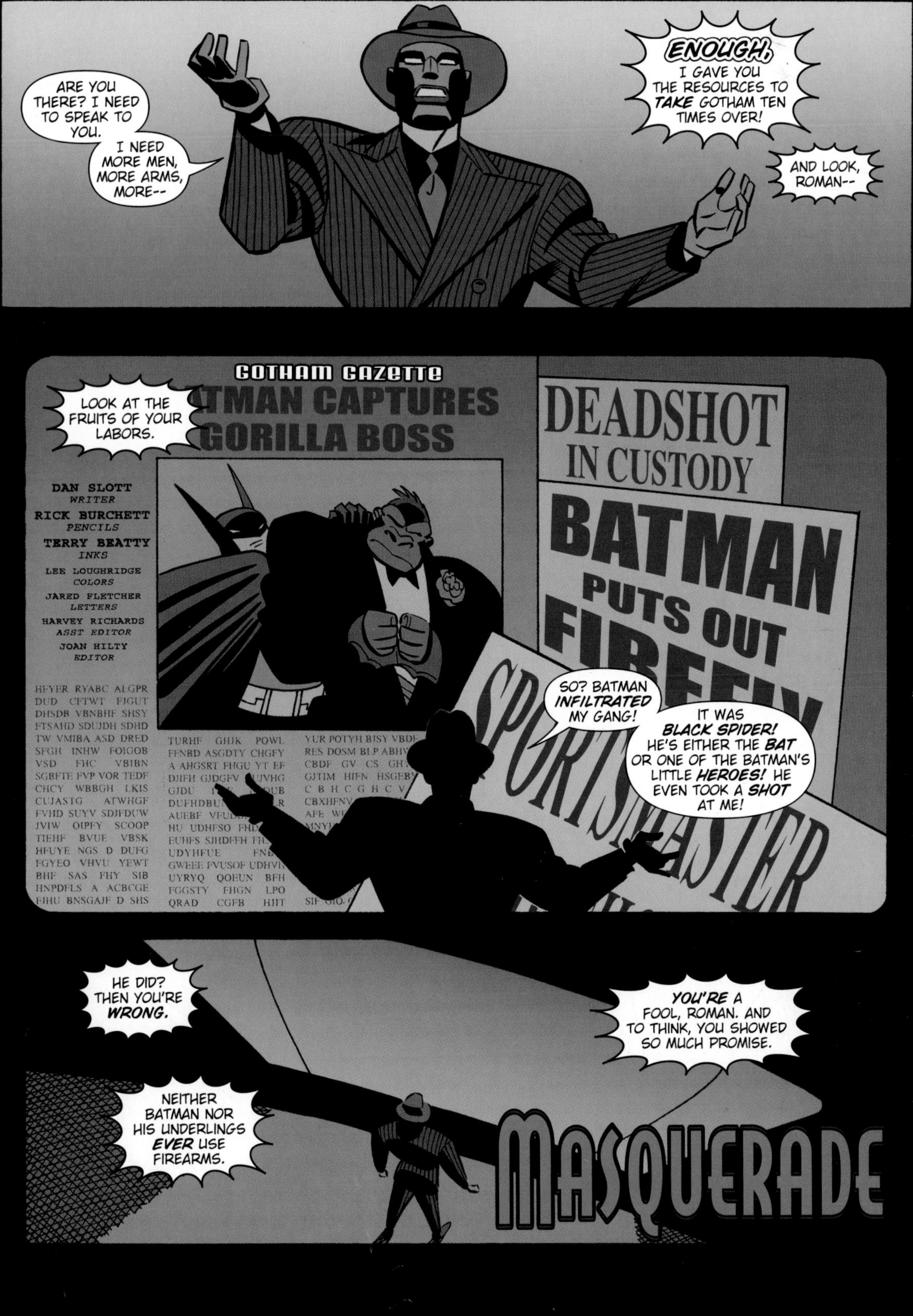
ARE YOU THERE? I NEED TO SPEAK TO YOU.
I NEED MORE MEN, MORE ARMS, MORE--
ENOUGH, I GAVE YOU THE RESOURCES TO TAKE GOTHAM TEN TIMES OVER!
AND LOOK, ROMAN--
GOTHAM GAZETTE
LOOK AT THE FRUITS OF YOUR LABORS.
ATMAN CAPTURES GORILLA BOSS
DAN SLOTT WRITER
RICK BURCHETT PENCILS
TERRY BEATTY INKS
LEE LOUGHRIDGE COLORS
JARED FLETCHER LETTERS
HARVEY RICHARDS ASST EDITOR
JOAN HILTY EDITOR
DEADSHOT IN CUSTODY
BATMAN PUTS OUT FIREFLY
SPORTSMASTER
SO? BATMAN INFILTRATED MY GANG!
IT WAS BLACK SPIDER! HE'S EITHER THE BAT OR ONE OF THE BATMAN'S LITTLE HEROES! HE EVEN TOOK A SHOT AT ME!
HE DID? THEN YOU'RE WRONG.
YOU'RE A FOOL, ROMAN. AND TO THINK, YOU SHOWED SO MUCH PROMISE.
NEITHER BATMAN NOR HIS UNDERLINGS EVER USE FIREARMS.
MASQUERADE

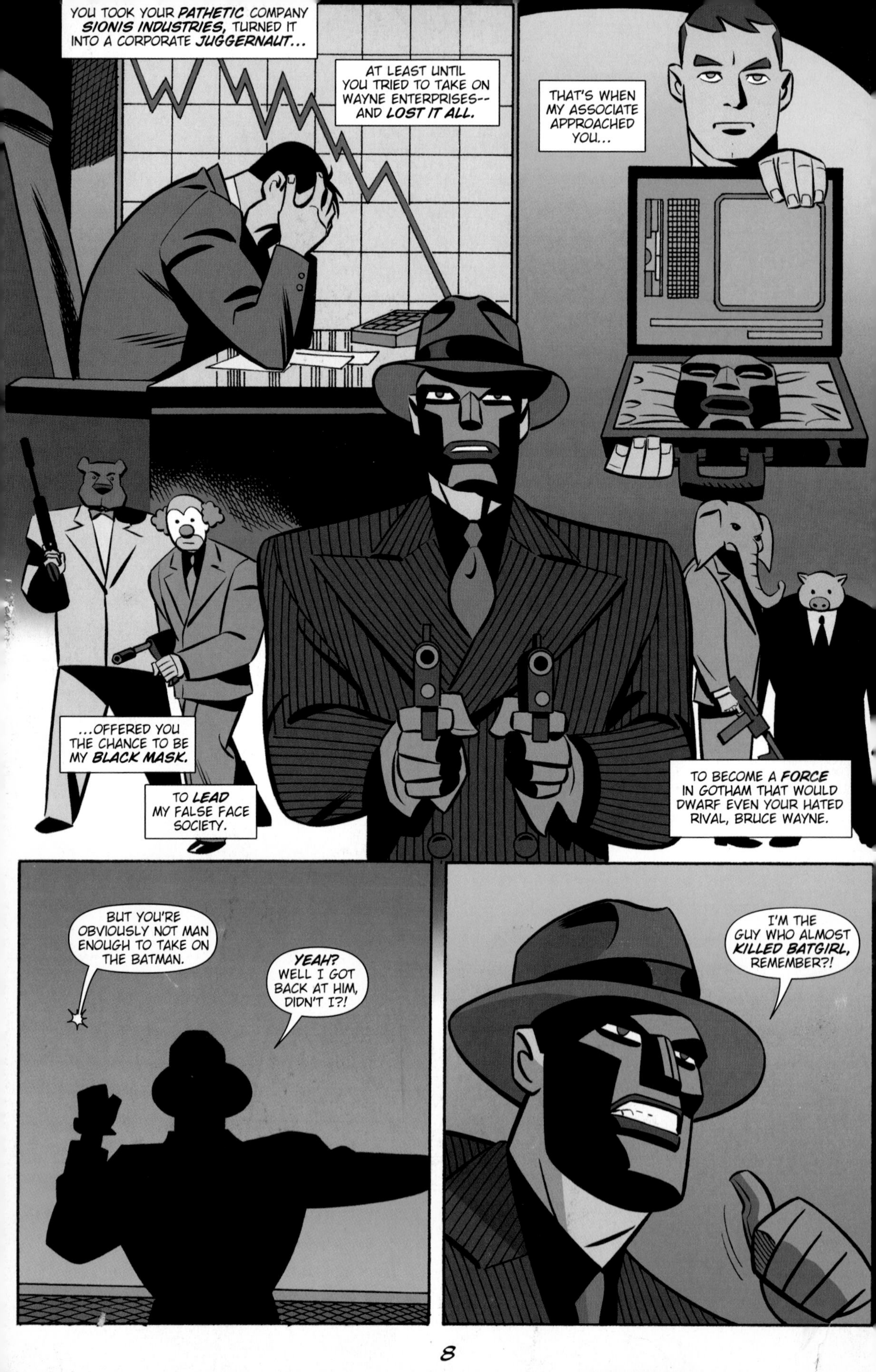
YOU TOOK YOUR PATHETIC COMPANY SIONIS INDUSTRIES, TURNED IT INTO A CORPORATE JUGGERNAUT...
AT LEAST UNTIL YOU TRIED TO TAKE ON WAYNE ENTERPRISES-- AND LOST IT ALL.
THAT'S WHEN MY ASSOCIATE APPROACHED YOU...
...OFFERED YOU THE CHANCE TO BE MY BLACK MASK.
TO LEAD MY FALSE FACE SOCIETY.
TO BECOME A FORCE IN GOTHAM THAT WOULD DWARF EVEN YOUR HATED RIVAL, BRUCE WAYNE.
BUT YOU'RE OBVIOUSLY NOT MAN ENOUGH TO TAKE ON THE BATMAN.
YEAH? WELL I GOT BACK AT HIM, DIDN'T I?!
I'M THE GUY WHO ALMOST KILLED BATGIRL, REMEMBER?!

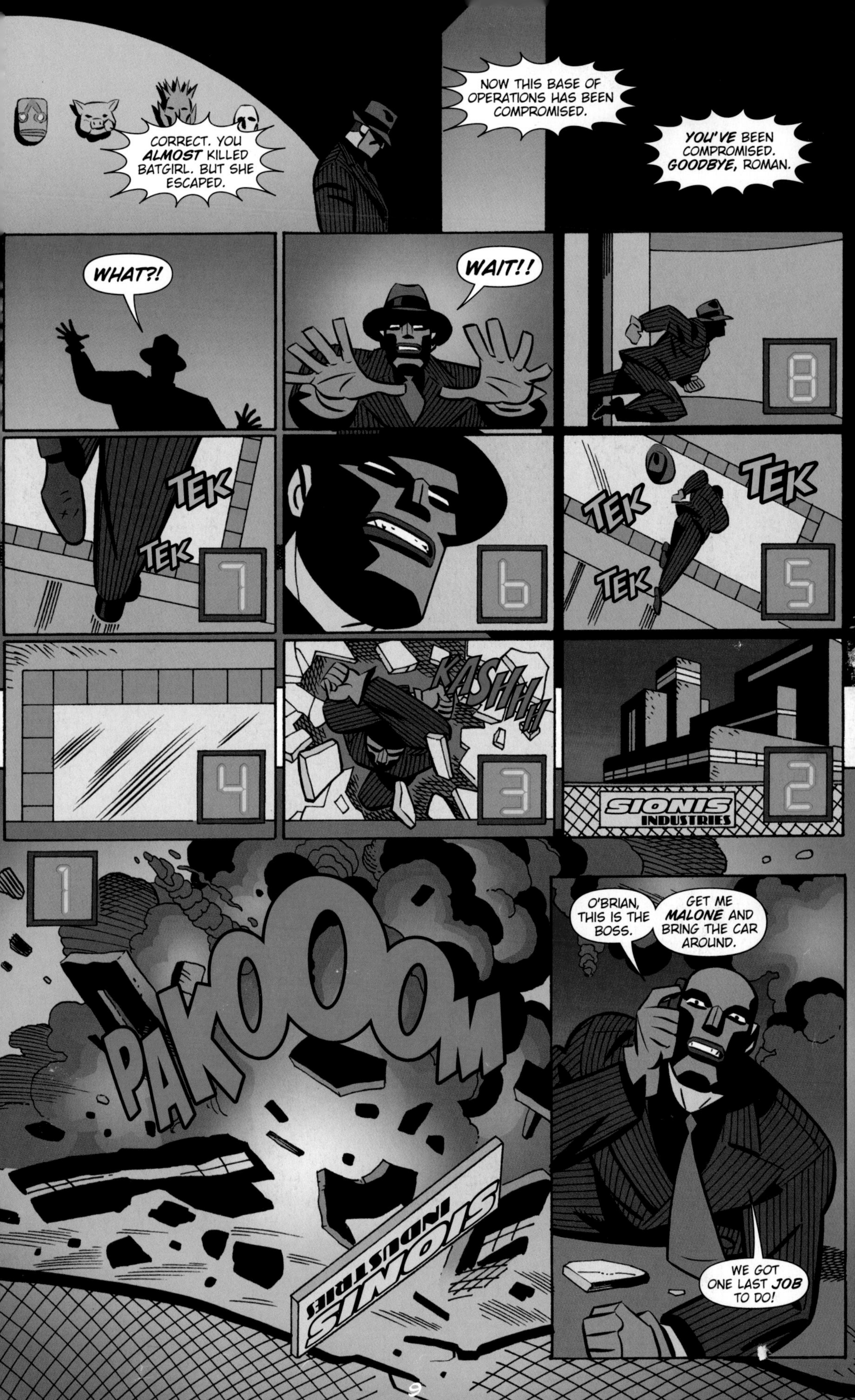
CORRECT. YOU ALMOST KILLED BATGIRL. BUT SHE ESCAPED.
NOW THIS BASE OF OPERATIONS HAS BEEN COMPROMISED.
YOU'VE BEEN COMPROMISED. GOODBYE, ROMAN.
WHAT?!
WAIT!!
8
TEK
TEK
7
6
TEK
TEK
TEK
5
4
KASHHH
3
SIONIS INDUSTRIES
2
1
PAKOOOM
SIONIS INDUSTRIES
O'BRIAN, THIS IS THE BOSS.
GET ME MALONE AND BRING THE CAR AROUND.
WE GOT ONE LAST JOB TO DO!

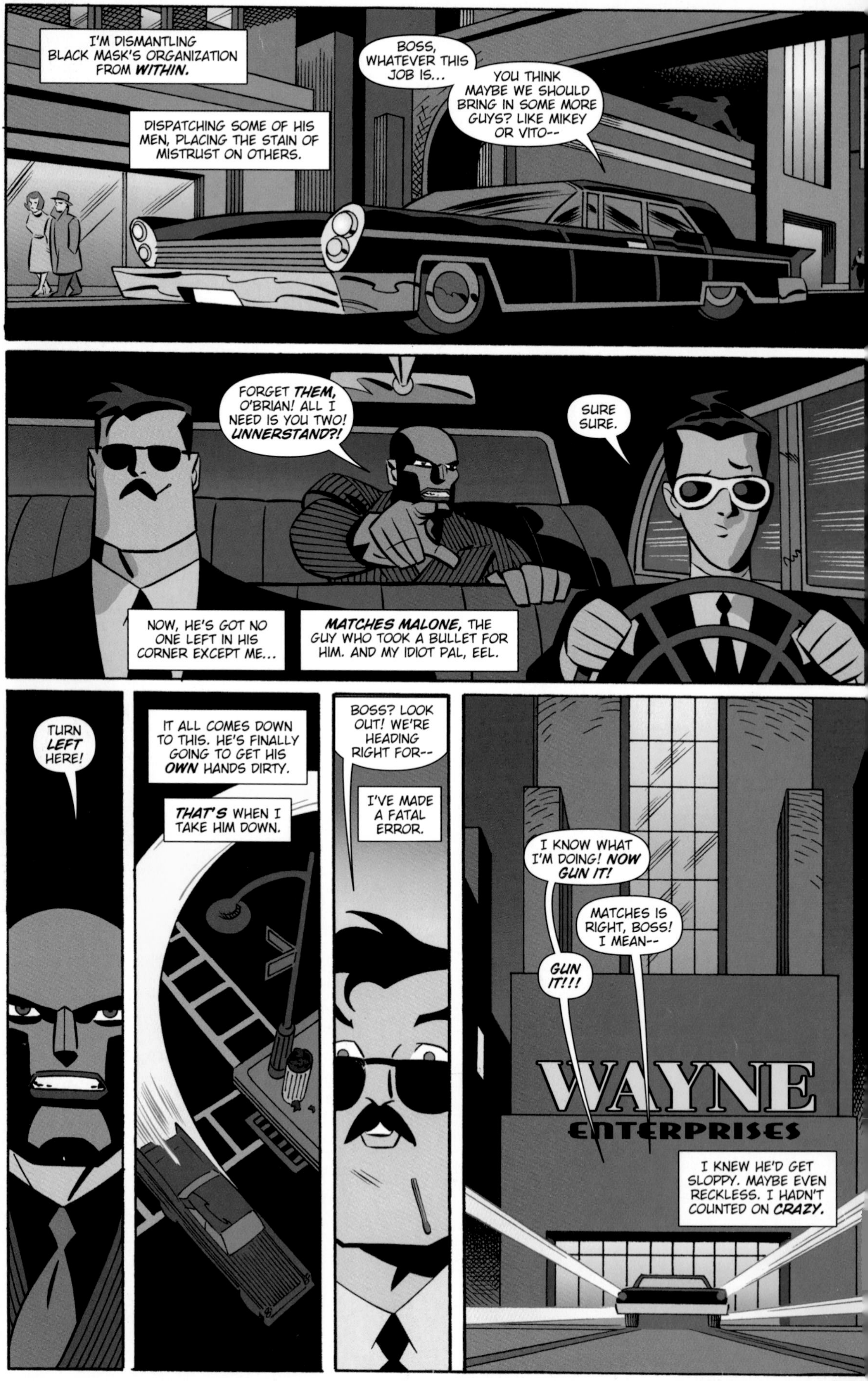
I'M DISMANTLING BLACK MASK'S ORGANIZATION FROM **WITHIN.**
DISPATCHING SOME OF HIS MEN, PLACING THE STAIN OF MISTRUST ON OTHERS.
BOSS, WHATEVER THIS JOB IS...
YOU THINK MAYBE WE SHOULD BRING IN SOME MORE GUYS? LIKE MIKEY OR VITO--
FORGET **THEM,** O'BRIAN! ALL I NEED IS YOU TWO! **UNNERSTAND?!**
SURE SURE.
NOW, HE'S GOT NO ONE LEFT IN HIS CORNER EXCEPT ME...
MATCHES MALONE, THE GUY WHO TOOK A BULLET FOR HIM. AND MY IDIOT PAL, EEL.
TURN **LEFT** HERE!
IT ALL COMES DOWN TO THIS. HE'S FINALLY GOING TO GET HIS **OWN** HANDS DIRTY.
THAT'S WHEN I TAKE HIM DOWN.
BOSS? LOOK OUT! WE'RE HEADING RIGHT FOR--
I'VE MADE A FATAL ERROR.
I KNOW WHAT I'M DOING! **NOW GUN IT!**
MATCHES IS RIGHT, BOSS! I MEAN--
GUN IT!!!
WAYNE ENTERPRISES
I KNEW HE'D GET SLOPPY. MAYBE EVEN RECKLESS. I HADN'T COUNTED ON **CRAZY.**

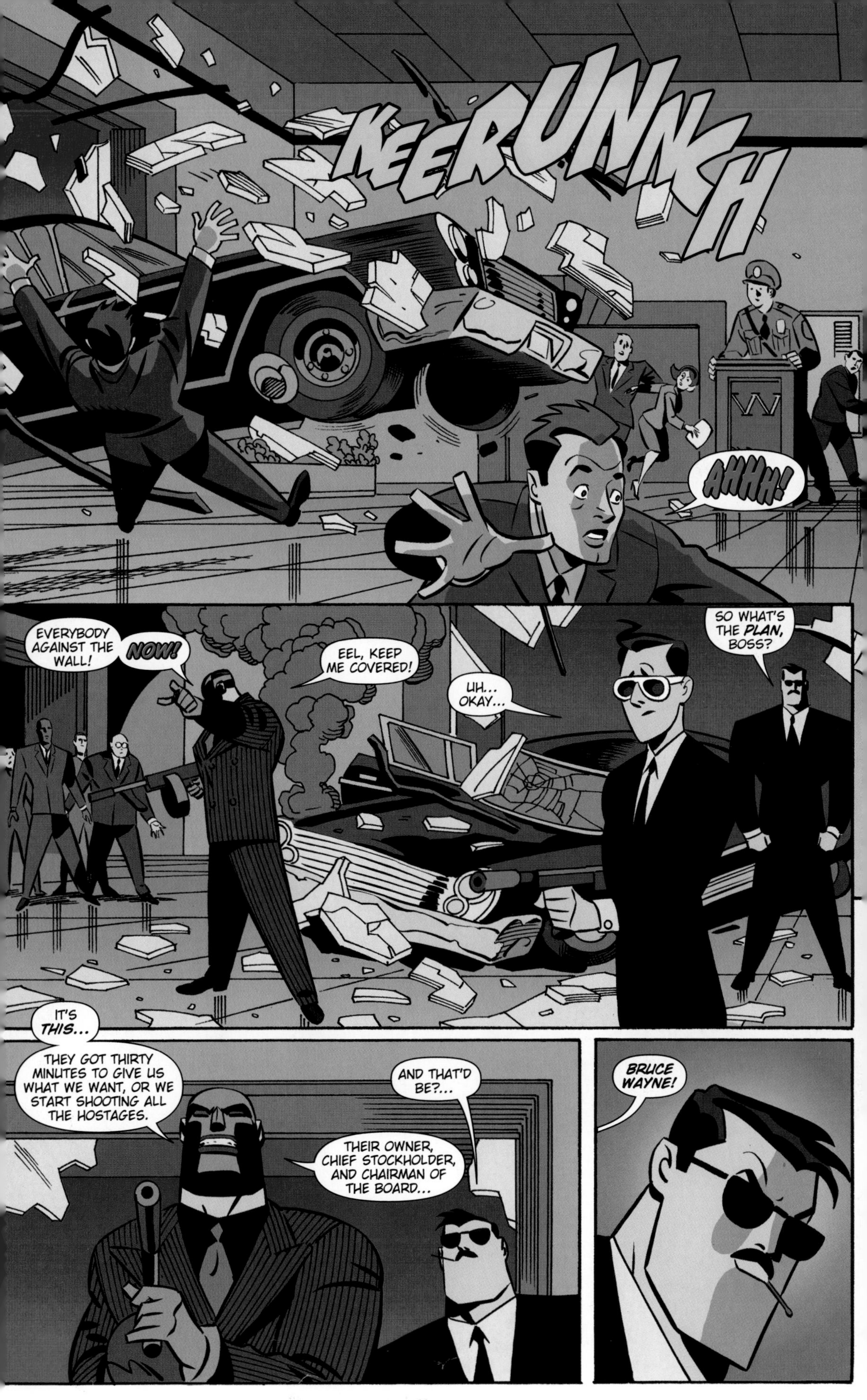
KEERUNNCH
AHHH!
EVERYBODY AGAINST THE WALL!
NOW!
EEL, KEEP ME COVERED!
UH... OKAY...
SO WHAT'S THE PLAN, BOSS?
IT'S THIS...
THEY GOT THIRTY MINUTES TO GIVE US WHAT WE WANT, OR WE START SHOOTING ALL THE HOSTAGES.
AND THAT'D BE?...
THEIR OWNER, CHIEF STOCKHOLDER, AND CHAIRMAN OF THE BOARD...
BRUCE WAYNE!

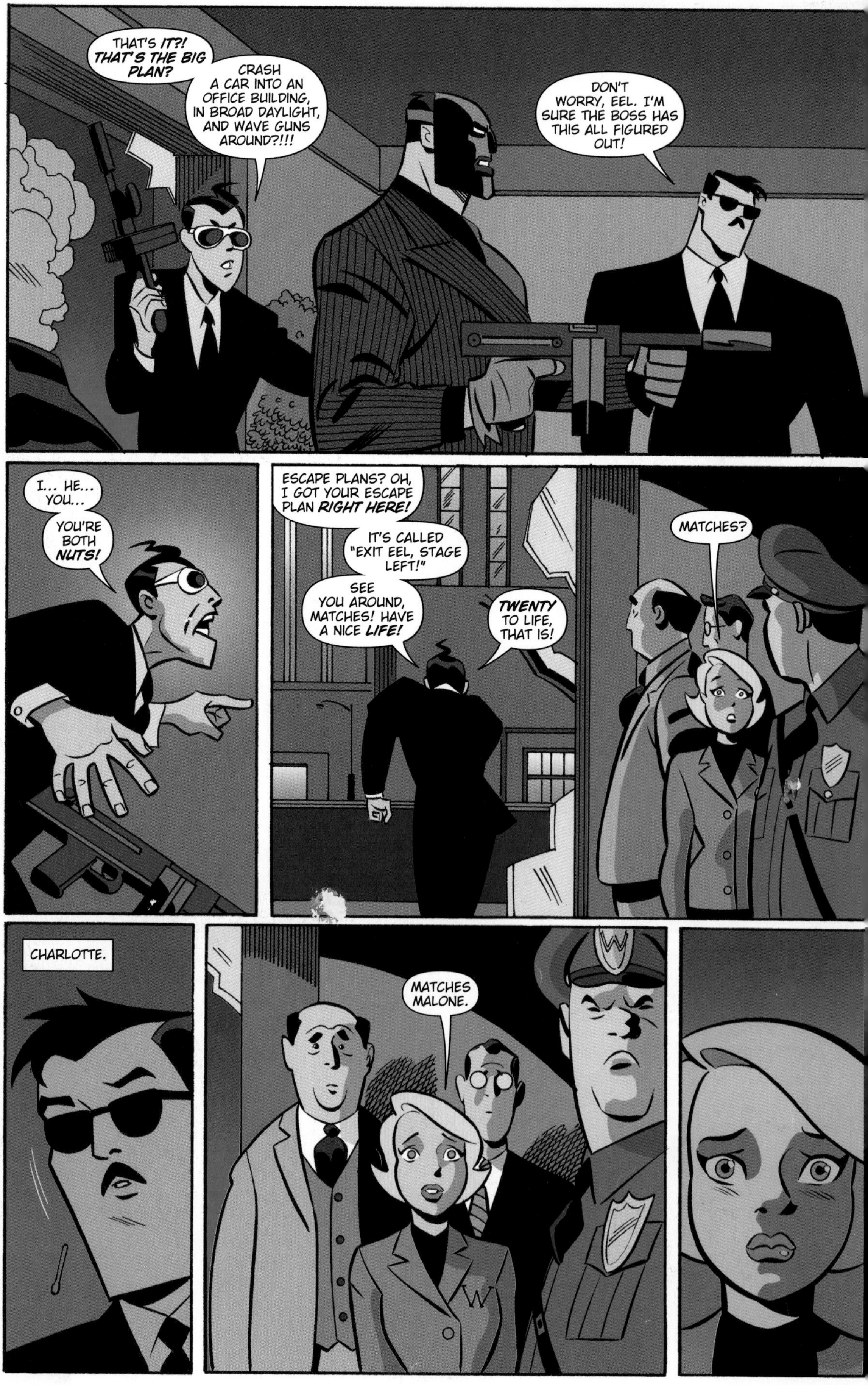
THAT'S *IT?!* ***THAT'S THE BIG PLAN?***
CRASH A CAR INTO AN OFFICE BUILDING, IN BROAD DAYLIGHT, AND WAVE GUNS AROUND?!!!
DON'T WORRY, EEL. I'M SURE THE BOSS HAS THIS ALL FIGURED OUT!
I... HE... YOU...
YOU'RE BOTH ***NUTS!***
ESCAPE PLANS? OH, I GOT YOUR ESCAPE PLAN ***RIGHT HERE!***
IT'S CALLED "EXIT EEL, STAGE LEFT!"
SEE YOU AROUND, MATCHES! HAVE A NICE ***LIFE!***
TWENTY TO LIFE, THAT IS!
MATCHES?
CHARLOTTE.
MATCHES MALONE.

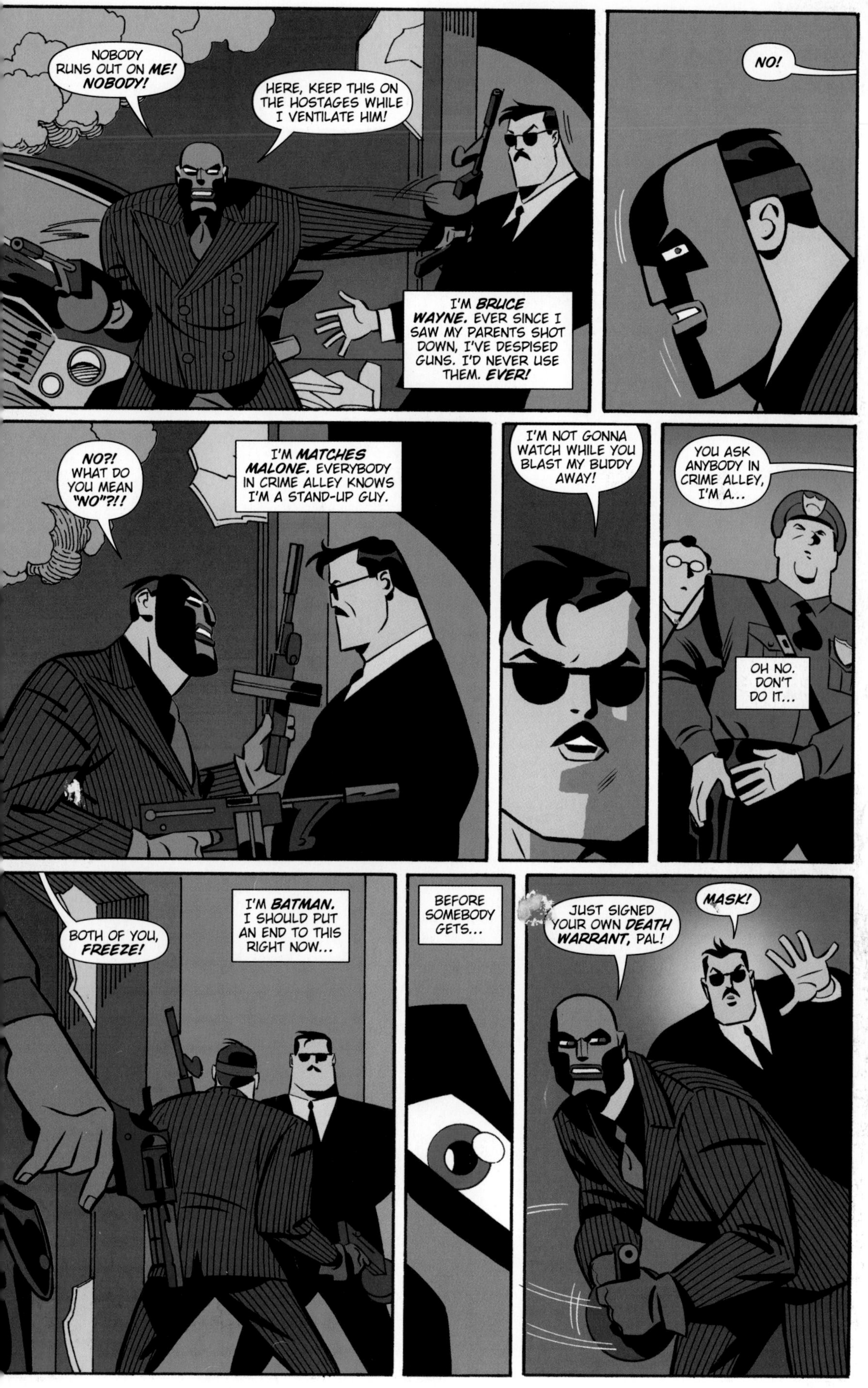
NOBODY RUNS OUT ON ME! NOBODY!
HERE, KEEP THIS ON THE HOSTAGES WHILE I VENTILATE HIM!
I'M BRUCE WAYNE. EVER SINCE I SAW MY PARENTS SHOT DOWN, I'VE DESPISED GUNS. I'D NEVER USE THEM. EVER!
NO!
NO?! WHAT DO YOU MEAN "NO"?!!
I'M MATCHES MALONE. EVERYBODY IN CRIME ALLEY KNOWS I'M A STAND-UP GUY.
I'M NOT GONNA WATCH WHILE YOU BLAST MY BUDDY AWAY!
YOU ASK ANYBODY IN CRIME ALLEY, I'M A...
OH NO. DON'T DO IT...
BOTH OF YOU, FREEZE!
I'M BATMAN. I SHOULD PUT AN END TO THIS RIGHT NOW...
BEFORE SOMEBODY GETS...
JUST SIGNED YOUR OWN DEATH WARRANT, PAL!
MASK!

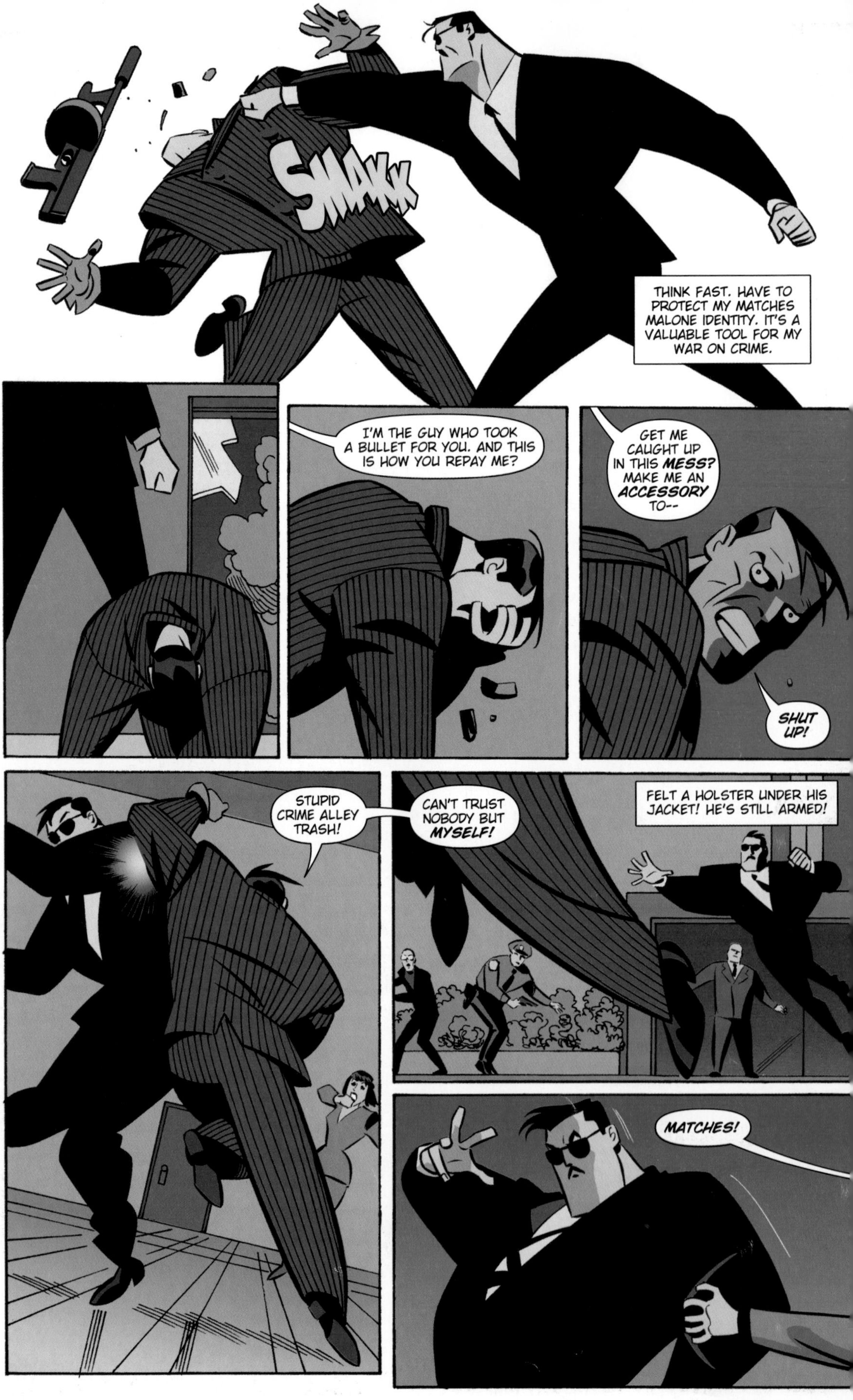
SMAKK
THINK FAST. HAVE TO PROTECT MY MATCHES MALONE IDENTITY. IT'S A VALUABLE TOOL FOR MY WAR ON CRIME.
I'M THE GUY WHO TOOK A BULLET FOR YOU. AND THIS IS HOW YOU REPAY ME?
GET ME CAUGHT UP IN THIS MESS? MAKE ME AN ACCESSORY TO--
SHUT UP!
STUPID CRIME ALLEY TRASH!
CAN'T TRUST NOBODY BUT MYSELF!
FELT A HOLSTER UNDER HIS JACKET! HE'S STILL ARMED!
MATCHES!

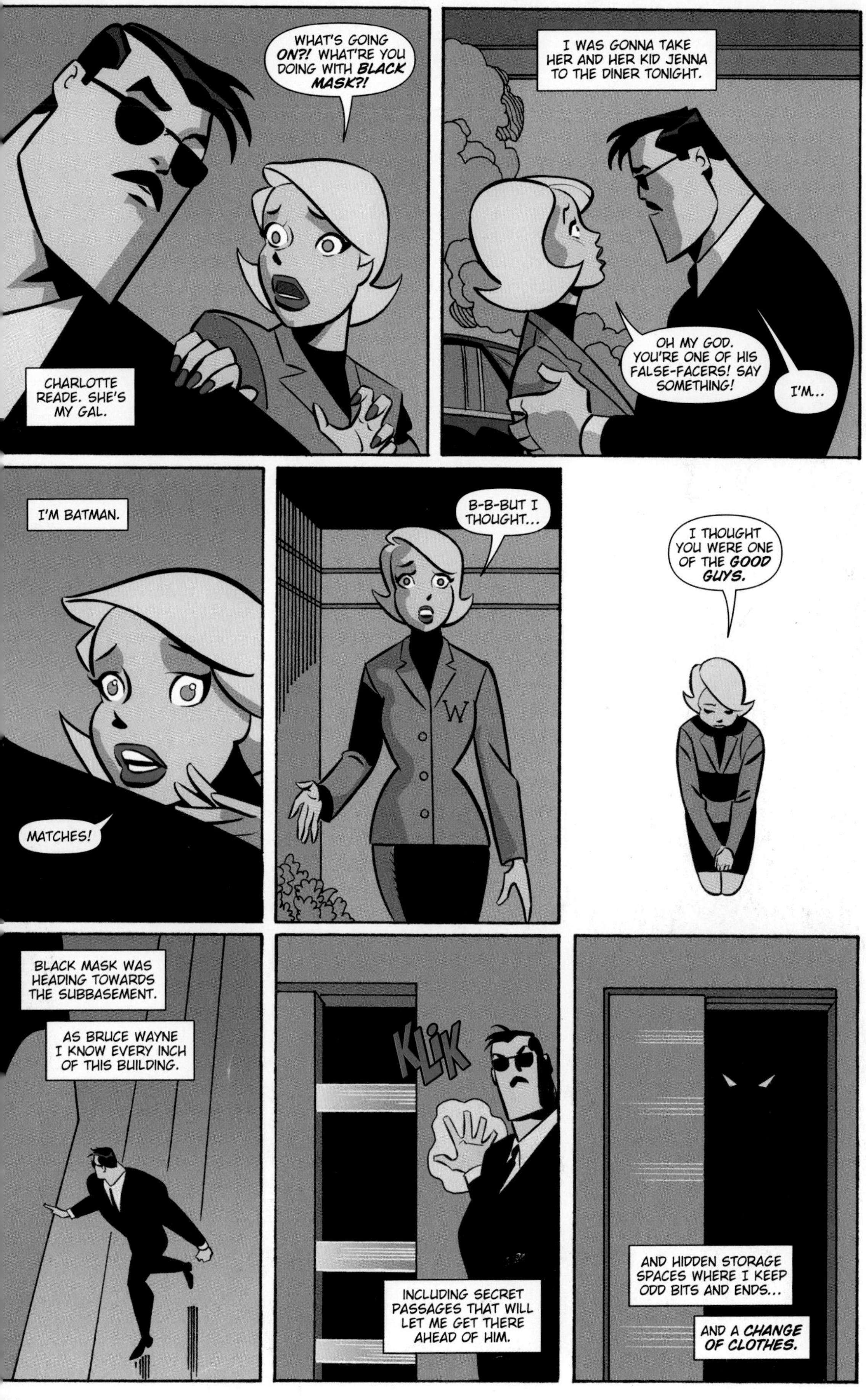
WHAT'S GOING ON?! WHAT'RE YOU DOING WITH BLACK MASK?!
CHARLOTTE READE. SHE'S MY GAL.
I WAS GONNA TAKE HER AND HER KID JENNA TO THE DINER TONIGHT.
OH MY GOD. YOU'RE ONE OF HIS FALSE-FACERS! SAY SOMETHING!
I'M...
I'M BATMAN.
MATCHES!
B-B-BUT I THOUGHT...
I THOUGHT YOU WERE ONE OF THE GOOD GUYS.
BLACK MASK WAS HEADING TOWARDS THE SUBBASEMENT.
AS BRUCE WAYNE I KNOW EVERY INCH OF THIS BUILDING.
KLIK
INCLUDING SECRET PASSAGES THAT WILL LET ME GET THERE AHEAD OF HIM.
AND HIDDEN STORAGE SPACES WHERE I KEEP ODD BITS AND ENDS...
AND A CHANGE OF CLOTHES.

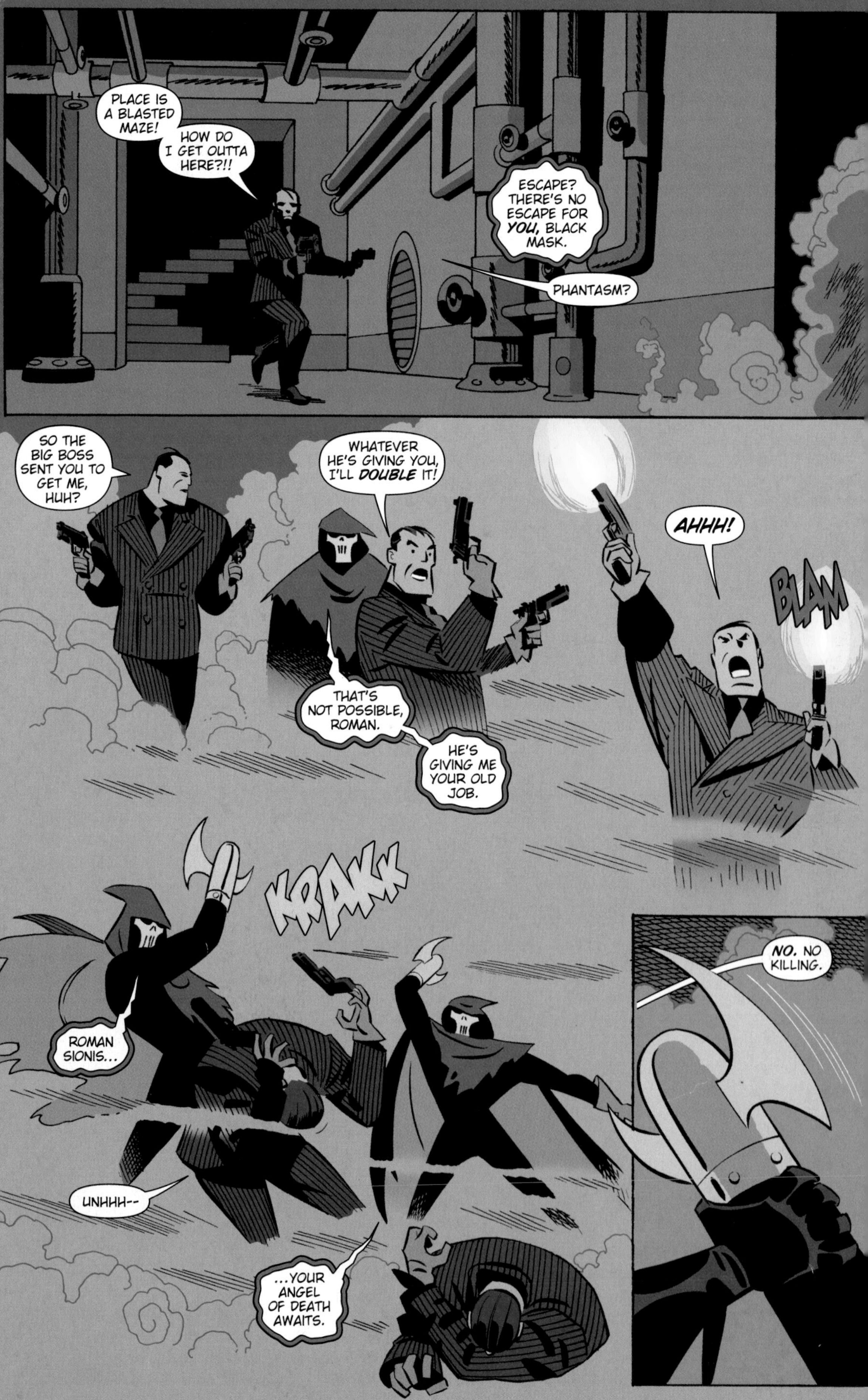

PLACE IS A BLASTED MAZE!
HOW DO I GET OUTTA HERE?!!
ESCAPE? THERE'S NO ESCAPE FOR *YOU*, BLACK MASK.
PHANTASM?
SO THE BIG BOSS SENT YOU TO GET ME, HUH?
WHATEVER HE'S GIVING YOU, I'LL *DOUBLE* IT!
THAT'S NOT POSSIBLE, ROMAN.
HE'S GIVING ME YOUR OLD JOB.
AHHH!
BLAM
KRAKK
ROMAN SIONIS...
UNHHH--
...YOUR ANGEL OF DEATH AWAITS.
NO. NO KILLING.

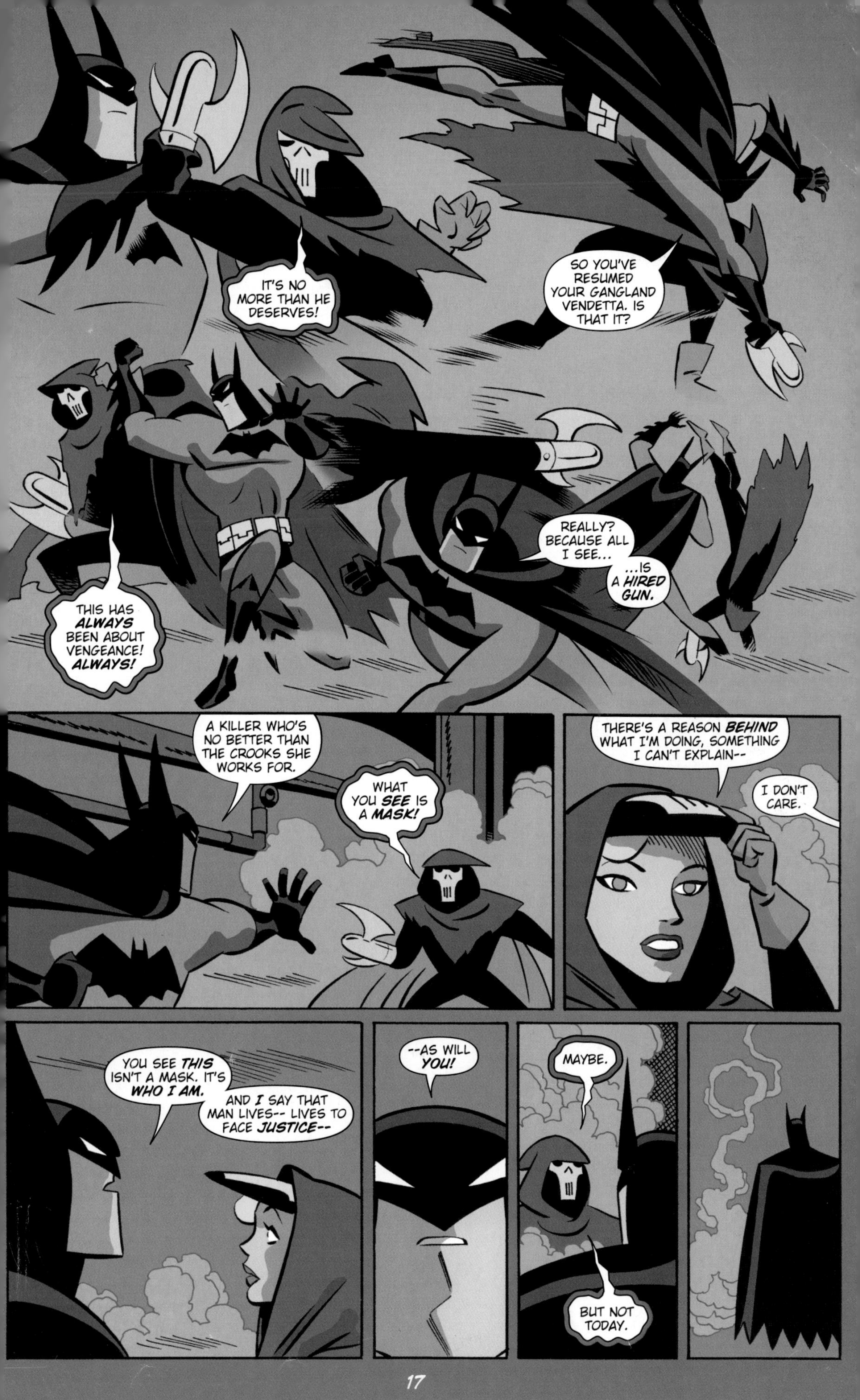
IT'S NO MORE THAN HE DESERVES!
SO YOU'VE RESUMED YOUR GANGLAND VENDETTA. IS THAT IT?
THIS HAS ALWAYS BEEN ABOUT VENGEANCE! ALWAYS!
REALLY? BECAUSE ALL I SEE...
...IS A HIRED GUN.
A KILLER WHO'S NO BETTER THAN THE CROOKS SHE WORKS FOR.
WHAT YOU SEE IS A MASK!
THERE'S A REASON BEHIND WHAT I'M DOING, SOMETHING I CAN'T EXPLAIN--
I DON'T CARE.
YOU SEE THIS ISN'T A MASK. IT'S WHO I AM.
AND I SAY THAT MAN LIVES-- LIVES TO FACE JUSTICE--
--AS WILL YOU!
MAYBE.
BUT NOT TODAY.

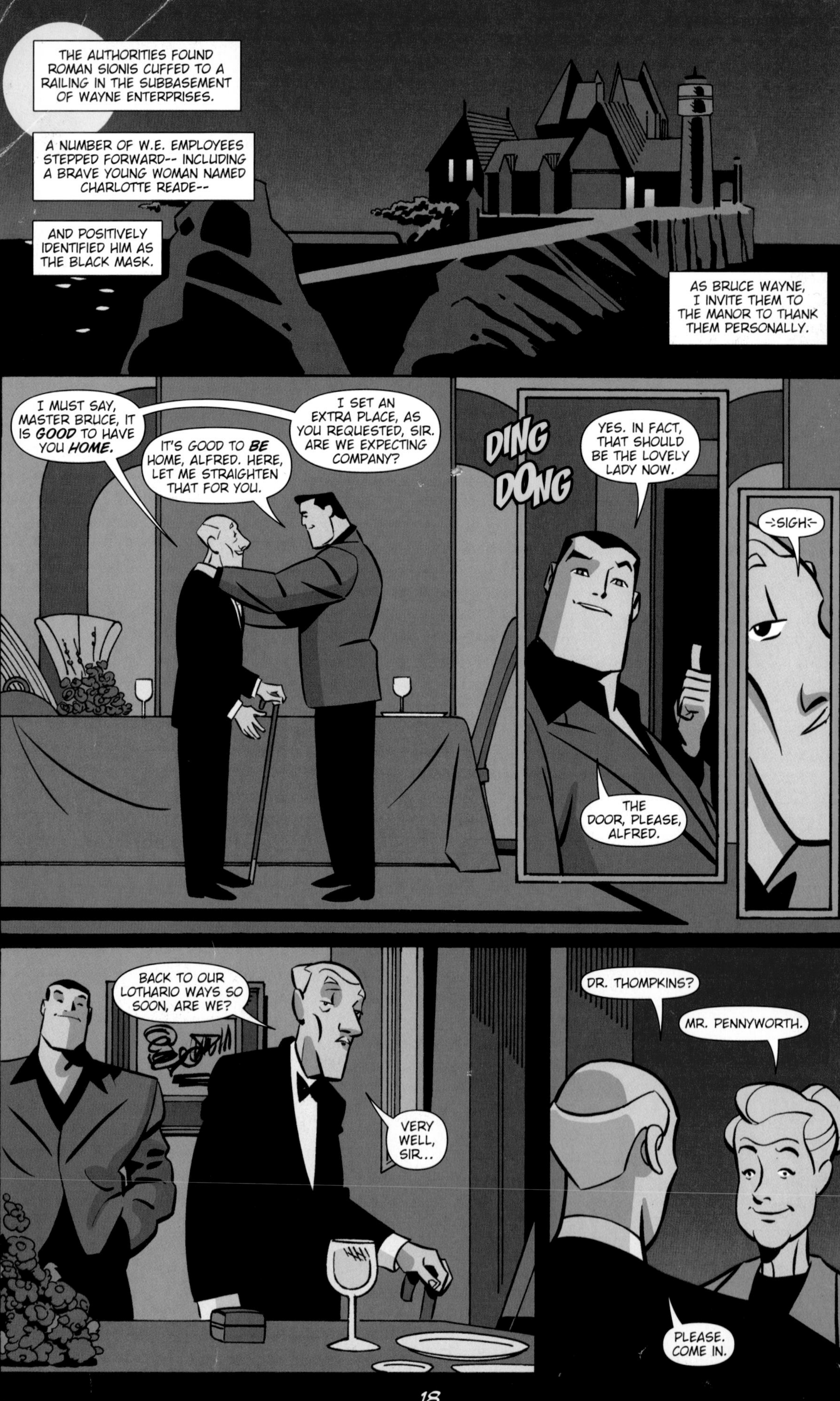
THE AUTHORITIES FOUND ROMAN SIONIS CUFFED TO A RAILING IN THE SUBBASEMENT OF WAYNE ENTERPRISES.
A NUMBER OF W.E. EMPLOYEES STEPPED FORWARD-- INCLUDING A BRAVE YOUNG WOMAN NAMED CHARLOTTE READE--
AND POSITIVELY IDENTIFIED HIM AS THE BLACK MASK.
AS BRUCE WAYNE, I INVITE THEM TO THE MANOR TO THANK THEM PERSONALLY.
I MUST SAY, MASTER BRUCE, IT IS GOOD TO HAVE YOU HOME.
IT'S GOOD TO BE HOME, ALFRED. HERE, LET ME STRAIGHTEN THAT FOR YOU.
I SET AN EXTRA PLACE, AS YOU REQUESTED, SIR. ARE WE EXPECTING COMPANY?
DING DONG
YES. IN FACT, THAT SHOULD BE THE LOVELY LADY NOW.
THE DOOR, PLEASE, ALFRED.
-:-SIGH-:-
BACK TO OUR LOTHARIO WAYS SO SOON, ARE WE?
VERY WELL, SIR..
DR. THOMPKINS?
MR. PENNYWORTH.
PLEASE. COME IN.

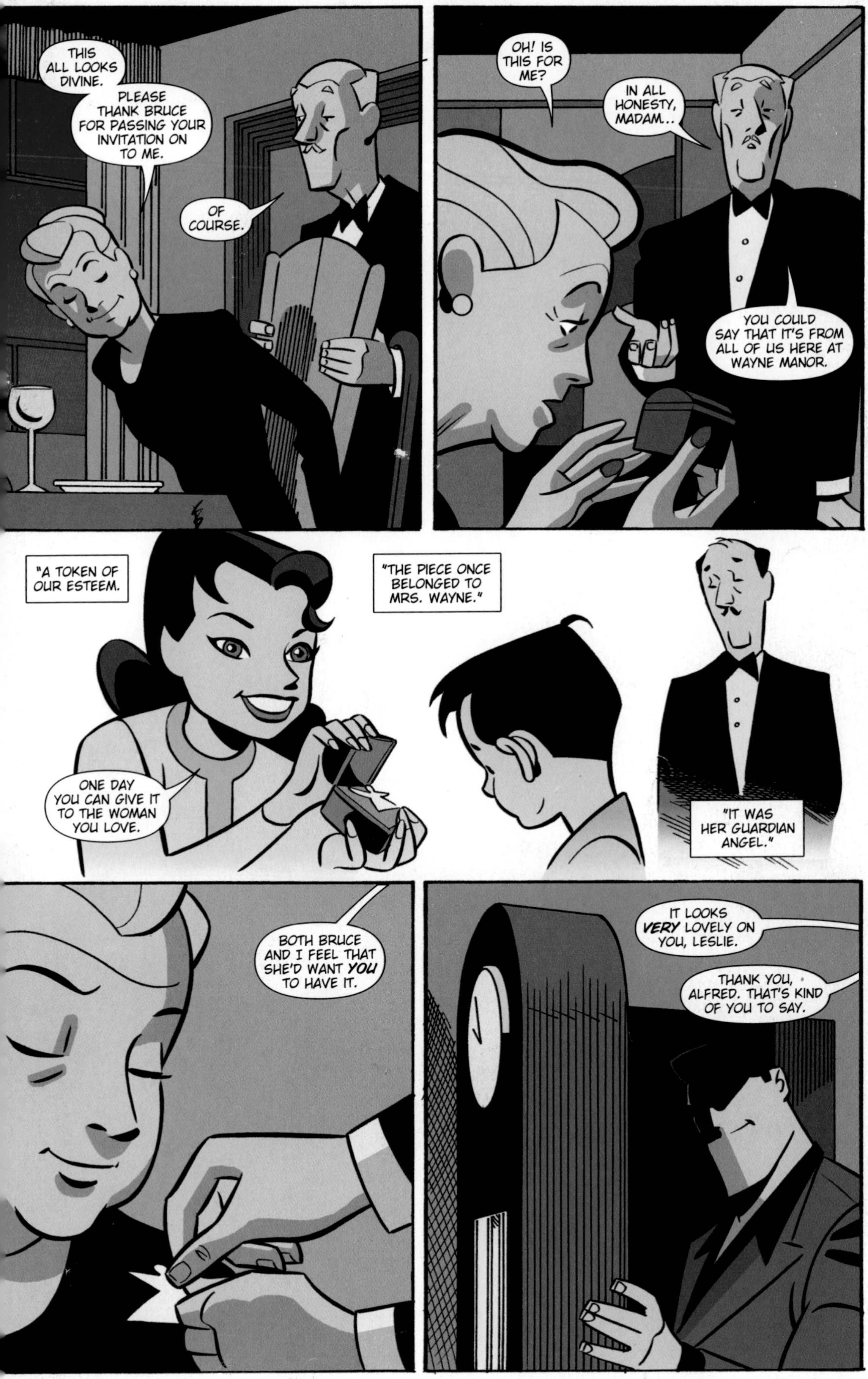
THIS ALL LOOKS DIVINE.
PLEASE THANK BRUCE FOR PASSING YOUR INVITATION ON TO ME.
OF COURSE.
OH! IS THIS FOR ME?
IN ALL HONESTY, MADAM..
YOU COULD SAY THAT IT'S FROM ALL OF US HERE AT WAYNE MANOR.
"A TOKEN OF OUR ESTEEM.
"THE PIECE ONCE BELONGED TO MRS. WAYNE."
ONE DAY YOU CAN GIVE IT TO THE WOMAN YOU LOVE.
"IT WAS HER GUARDIAN ANGEL."
BOTH BRUCE AND I FEEL THAT SHE'D WANT YOU TO HAVE IT.
IT LOOKS VERY LOVELY ON YOU, LESLIE.
THANK YOU, ALFRED. THAT'S KIND OF YOU TO SAY.

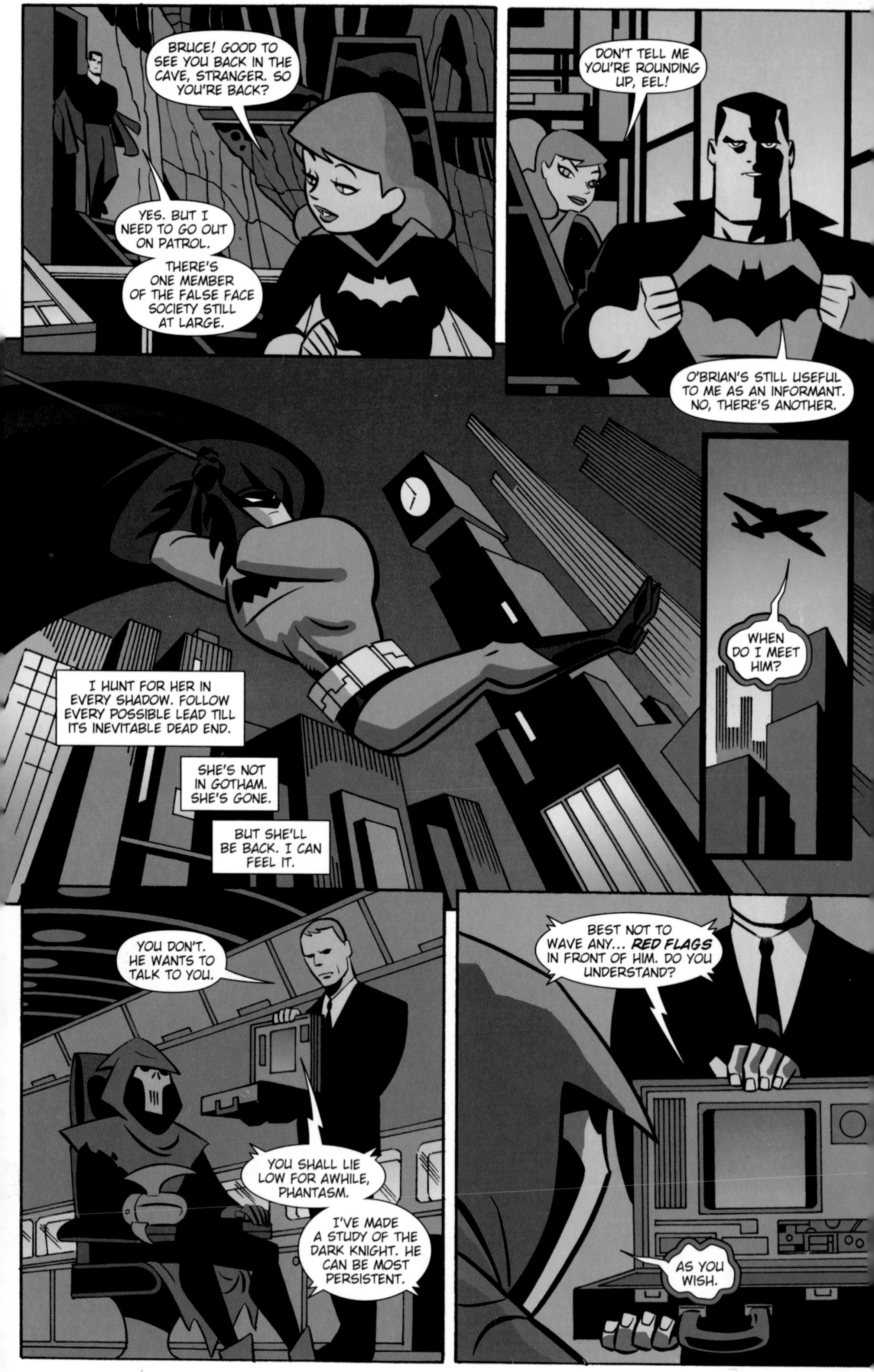
BRUCE! GOOD TO SEE YOU BACK IN THE CAVE, STRANGER. SO YOU'RE BACK?
YES. BUT I NEED TO GO OUT ON PATROL.
THERE'S ONE MEMBER OF THE FALSE FACE SOCIETY STILL AT LARGE.
DON'T TELL ME YOU'RE ROUNDING UP, EEL!
O'BRIAN'S STILL USEFUL TO ME AS AN INFORMANT. NO, THERE'S ANOTHER.
I HUNT FOR HER IN EVERY SHADOW. FOLLOW EVERY POSSIBLE LEAD TILL ITS INEVITABLE DEAD END.
SHE'S NOT IN GOTHAM. SHE'S GONE.
BUT SHE'LL BE BACK. I CAN FEEL IT.
WHEN DO I MEET HIM?
YOU DON'T. HE WANTS TO TALK TO YOU.
YOU SHALL LIE LOW FOR AWHILE, PHANTASM.
I'VE MADE A STUDY OF THE DARK KNIGHT. HE CAN BE MOST PERSISTENT.
BEST NOT TO WAVE ANY... **RED FLAGS** IN FRONT OF HIM. DO YOU UNDERSTAND?
AS YOU WISH.

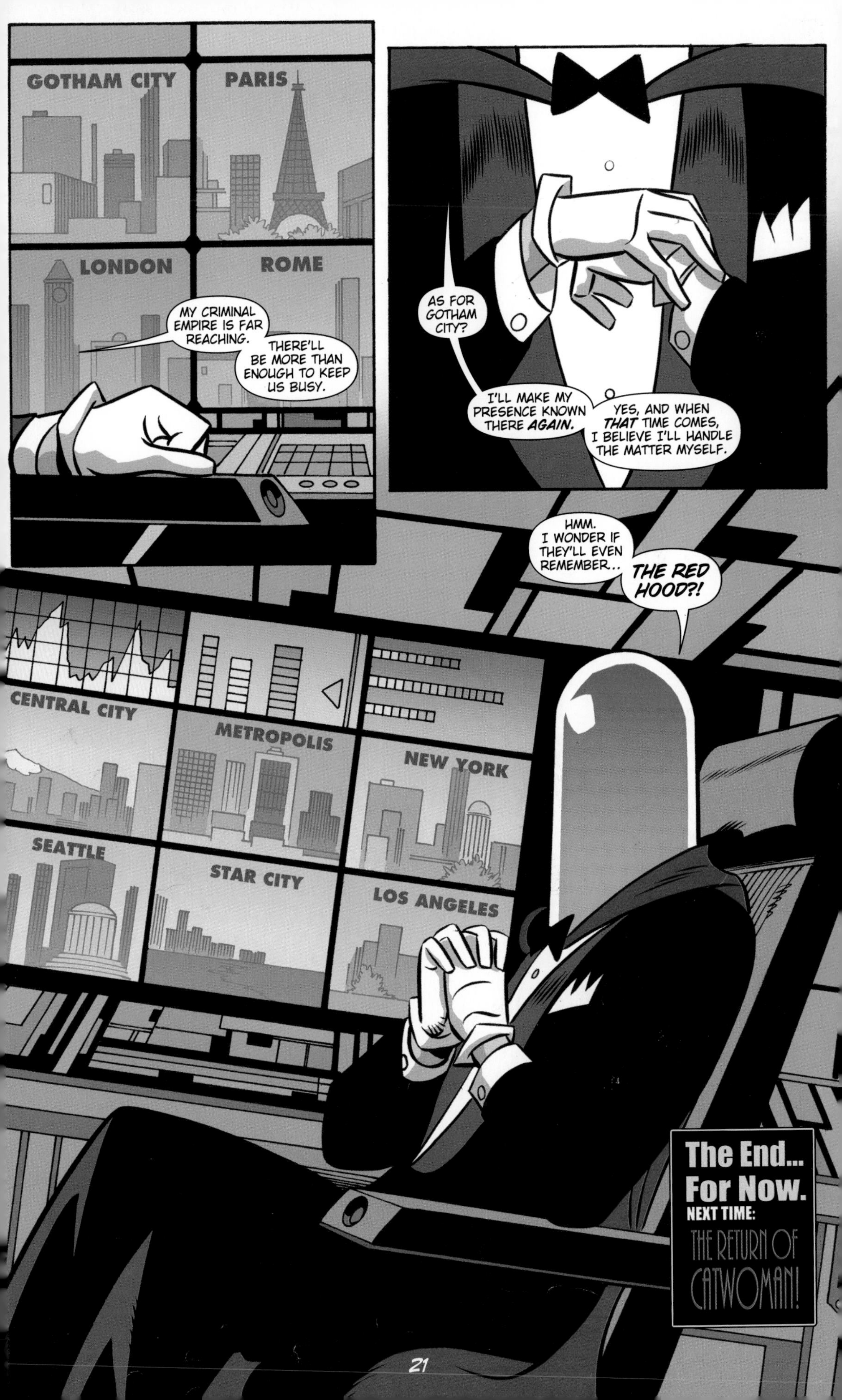
GOTHAM CITY
PARIS
LONDON
ROME
MY CRIMINAL EMPIRE IS FAR REACHING.
THERE'LL BE MORE THAN ENOUGH TO KEEP US BUSY.
AS FOR GOTHAM CITY?
I'LL MAKE MY PRESENCE KNOWN THERE AGAIN.
YES, AND WHEN THAT TIME COMES, I BELIEVE I'LL HANDLE THE MATTER MYSELF.
HMM. I WONDER IF THEY'LL EVEN REMEMBER..
THE RED HOOD?!
CENTRAL CITY
METROPOLIS
NEW YORK
SEATTLE
STAR CITY
LOS ANGELES
The End... For Now.
NEXT TIME:
THE RETURN OF CATWOMAN!

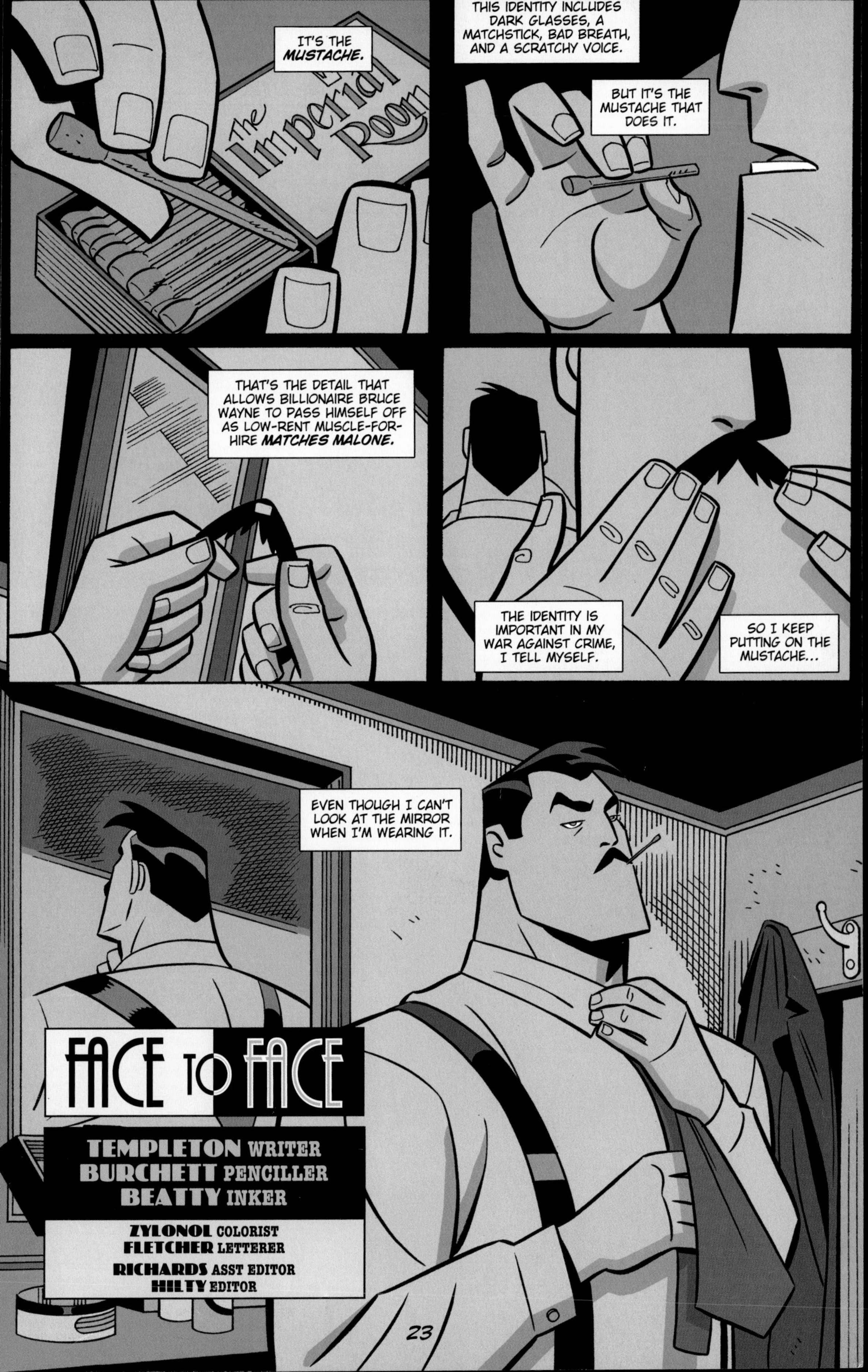
IT'S THE MUSTACHE.
The Imperial Room
THIS IDENTITY INCLUDES DARK GLASSES, A MATCHSTICK, BAD BREATH, AND A SCRATCHY VOICE.
BUT IT'S THE MUSTACHE THAT DOES IT.
THAT'S THE DETAIL THAT ALLOWS BILLIONAIRE BRUCE WAYNE TO PASS HIMSELF OFF AS LOW-RENT MUSCLE-FOR-HIRE MATCHES MALONE.
THE IDENTITY IS IMPORTANT IN MY WAR AGAINST CRIME, I TELL MYSELF.
SO I KEEP PUTTING ON THE MUSTACHE...
EVEN THOUGH I CAN'T LOOK AT THE MIRROR WHEN I'M WEARING IT.
FACE TO FACE
TEMPLETON WRITER
BURCHETT PENCILLER
BEATTY INKER
ZYLONOL COLORIST
FLETCHER LETTERER
RICHARDS ASST EDITOR
HILTY EDITOR

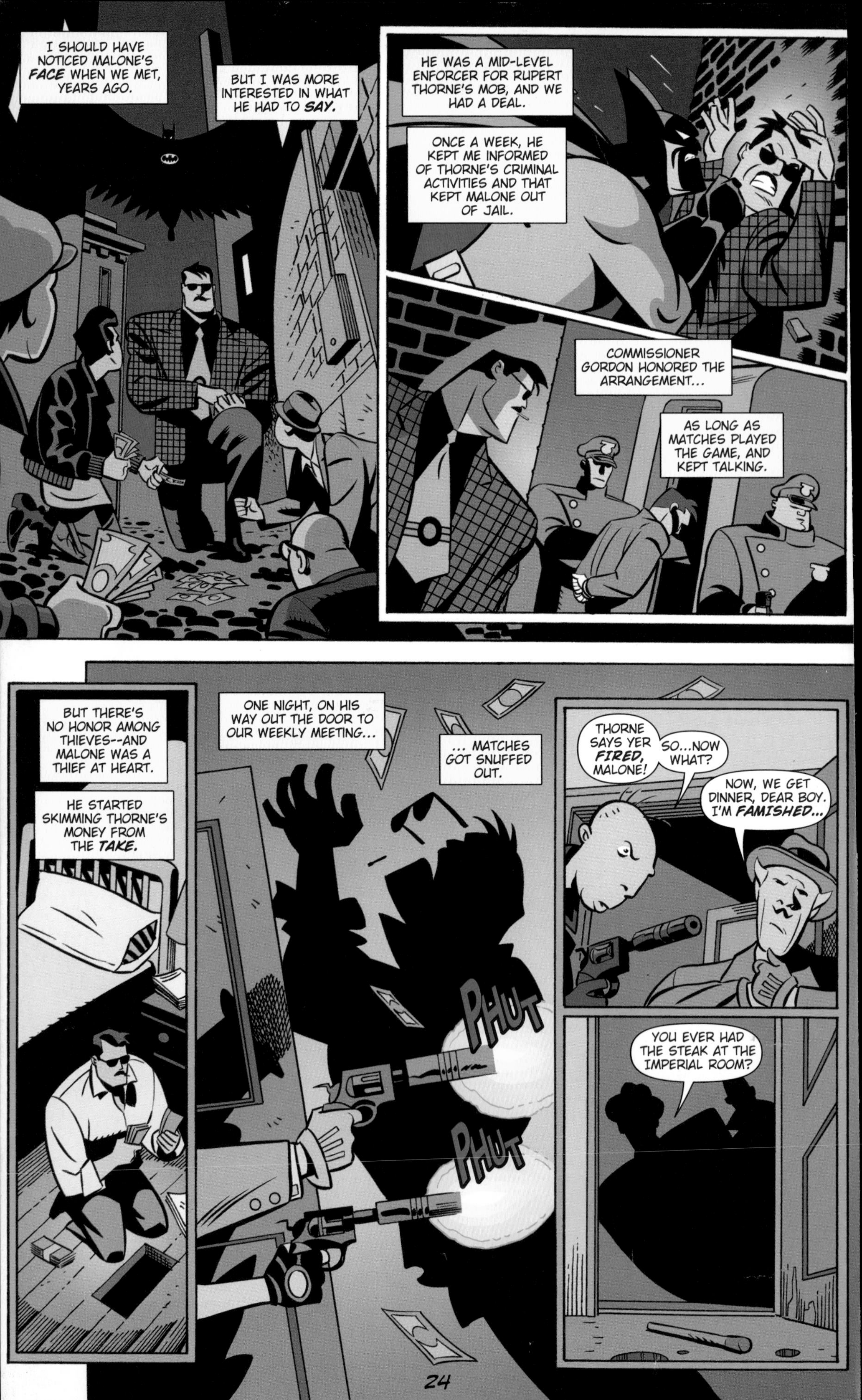

I SHOULD HAVE NOTICED MALONE'S *FACE* WHEN WE MET, YEARS AGO.
BUT I WAS MORE INTERESTED IN WHAT HE HAD TO *SAY.*
HE WAS A MID-LEVEL ENFORCER FOR RUPERT THORNE'S MOB, AND WE HAD A DEAL.
ONCE A WEEK, HE KEPT ME INFORMED OF THORNE'S CRIMINAL ACTIVITIES AND THAT KEPT MALONE OUT OF JAIL.
COMMISSIONER GORDON HONORED THE ARRANGEMENT...
AS LONG AS MATCHES PLAYED THE GAME, AND KEPT TALKING.
BUT THERE'S NO HONOR AMONG THIEVES--AND MALONE WAS A THIEF AT HEART.
HE STARTED SKIMMING THORNE'S MONEY FROM THE *TAKE.*
ONE NIGHT, ON HIS WAY OUT THE DOOR TO OUR WEEKLY MEETING...
... MATCHES GOT SNUFFED OUT.
PHUT
PHUT
THORNE SAYS YER *FIRED,* MALONE!
SO...NOW WHAT?
NOW, WE GET DINNER, DEAR BOY. I'M *FAMISHED...*
YOU EVER HAD THE STEAK AT THE IMPERIAL ROOM?

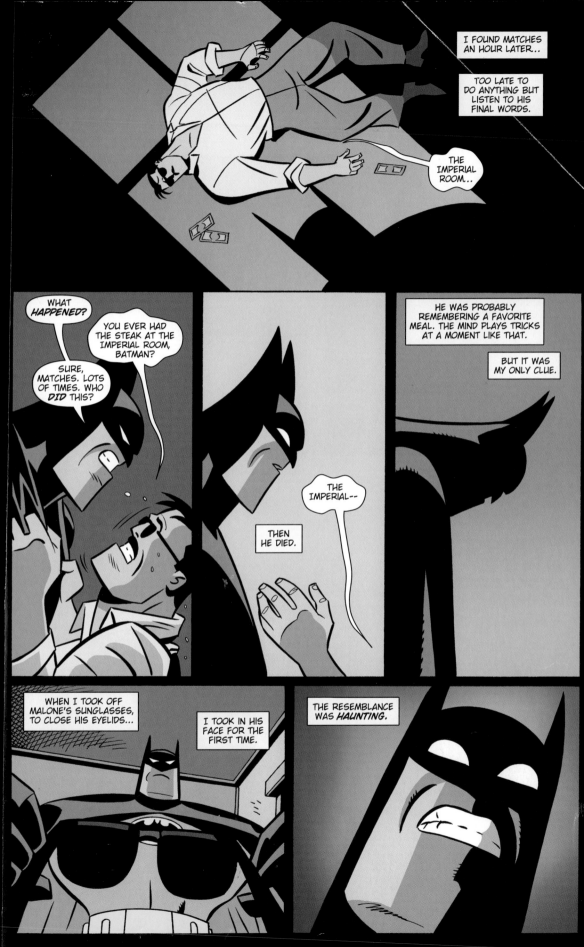

I FOUND MATCHES AN HOUR LATER...

TOO LATE TO DO ANYTHING BUT LISTEN TO HIS FINAL WORDS.

THE IMPERIAL ROOM...

WHAT *HAPPENED?*

YOU EVER HAD THE STEAK AT THE IMPERIAL ROOM, BATMAN?

SURE, MATCHES. LOTS OF TIMES. WHO *DID* THIS?

THE IMPERIAL--

THEN HE DIED.

HE WAS PROBABLY REMEMBERING A FAVORITE MEAL. THE MIND PLAYS TRICKS AT A MOMENT LIKE THAT.

BUT IT WAS MY ONLY CLUE.

WHEN I TOOK OFF MALONE'S SUNGLASSES, TO CLOSE HIS EYELIDS...

I TOOK IN HIS FACE FOR THE FIRST TIME.

THE RESEMBLANCE WAS *HAUNTING.*

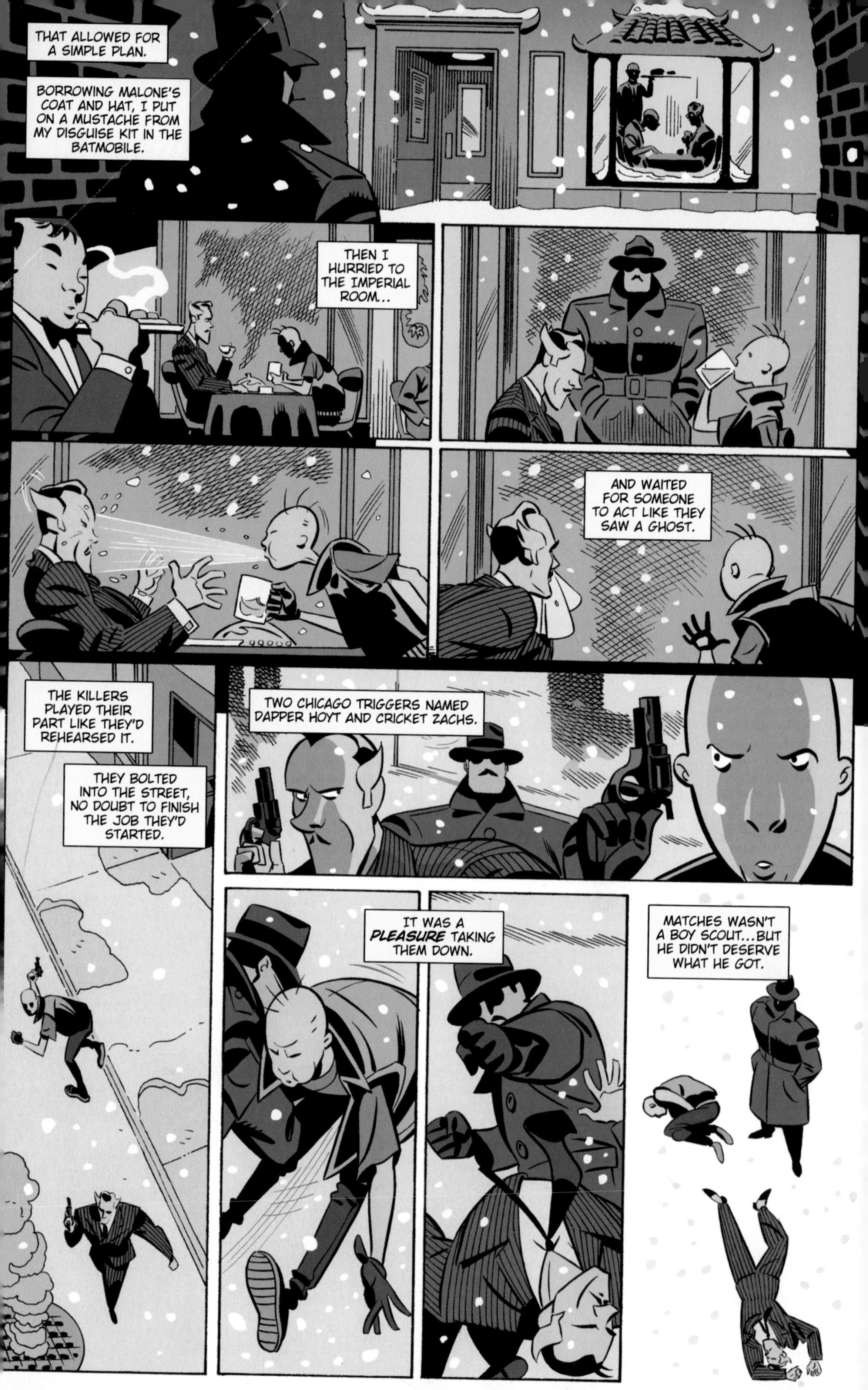
THAT ALLOWED FOR A SIMPLE PLAN.
BORROWING MALONE'S COAT AND HAT, I PUT ON A MUSTACHE FROM MY DISGUISE KIT IN THE BATMOBILE.
THEN I HURRIED TO THE IMPERIAL ROOM...
AND WAITED FOR SOMEONE TO ACT LIKE THEY SAW A GHOST.
THE KILLERS PLAYED THEIR PART LIKE THEY'D REHEARSED IT.
THEY BOLTED INTO THE STREET, NO DOUBT TO FINISH THE JOB THEY'D STARTED.
TWO CHICAGO TRIGGERS NAMED DAPPER HOYT AND CRICKET ZACHS.
IT WAS A PLEASURE TAKING THEM DOWN.
MATCHES WASN'T A BOY SCOUT...BUT HE DIDN'T DESERVE WHAT HE GOT.

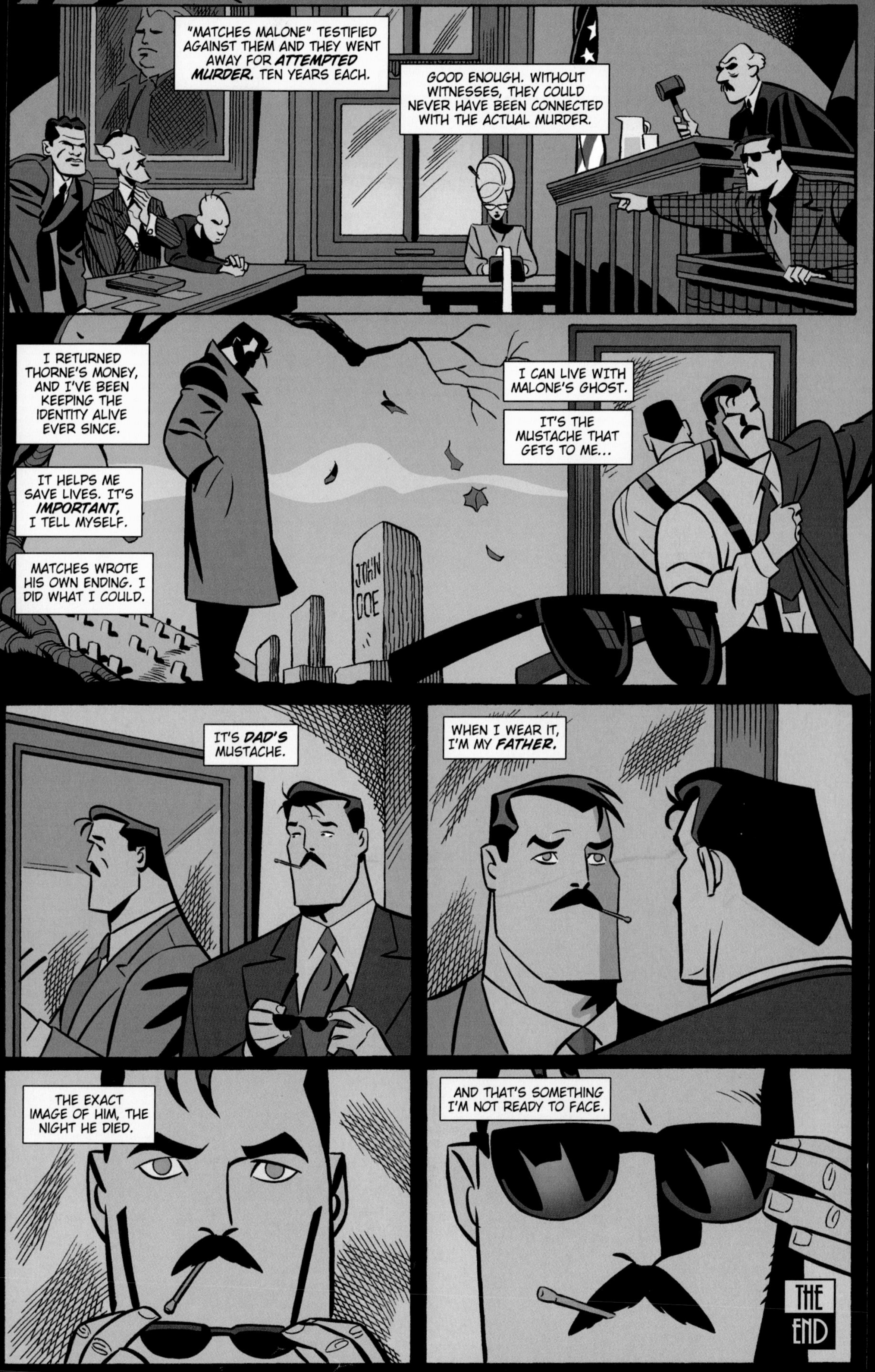
"MATCHES MALONE" TESTIFIED AGAINST THEM AND THEY WENT AWAY FOR ATTEMPTED MURDER. TEN YEARS EACH.
GOOD ENOUGH. WITHOUT WITNESSES, THEY COULD NEVER HAVE BEEN CONNECTED WITH THE ACTUAL MURDER.
I RETURNED THORNE'S MONEY, AND I'VE BEEN KEEPING THE IDENTITY ALIVE EVER SINCE.
IT HELPS ME SAVE LIVES. IT'S IMPORTANT, I TELL MYSELF.
MATCHES WROTE HIS OWN ENDING. I DID WHAT I COULD.
JOHN DOE
I CAN LIVE WITH MALONE'S GHOST.
IT'S THE MUSTACHE THAT GETS TO ME...
IT'S DAD'S MUSTACHE.
WHEN I WEAR IT, I'M MY FATHER.
THE EXACT IMAGE OF HIM, THE NIGHT HE DIED.
AND THAT'S SOMETHING I'M NOT READY TO FACE.
THE END

CREATORS

DAN SLOTT WRITER

Dan Slott is a comics writer best known for his work on DC Comics' Arkham Asylum, and, for Marvel, The Avengers and the Amazing Spider-Man.

RICK BURCHETT PENCILLER

Rick Burchett has worked as a comics artist for more than 25 years. He has received the comics industry's Eisner Award three times, Spain's Haxtur Award, and he has been nominated for the Eagle Award. Rick lives with his wife and two sons in Missouri, USA.

TERRY BEATTY INKER

For more than ten years, Terry Beatty was the main inker of DC Comics' "animated-style" Batman comics, including The Batman Strikes. More recently, he worked on *Return to Perdition*, a graphic novel for DC's Vertigo Crime.

LEE LOUGHRIDGE COLORIST

Lee Loughridge has been working in comics for more than fifteen years. He currently lives in sunny California in a tent on the beach.

GLOSSARY

accessory (ak-SESS-uh-ree)--an accessory to a crime is someone who helps another person commit a crime or helps cover up a crime by not reporting it

compromised (KOM-pruh-mized)--exposed a secret or made someone vulnerable

dismantle (diss-MAN-tuhl)--take apart piece by piece

famished (FAM-isht)--very hungry

inevitable (in-EV-uh-tuh-buhl)--sure to happen

infiltrate (IN-fil-trate)--join an enemy's side secretly in order to spy or cause some sort of damage

juggernaut (JUHG-ur-nawt)--a very powerful force that can destroy anything in its path

resemblance (ri-ZEM-bluhnss)--the appearance of looking like someone or something

rival (RYE-vuhl)--an opponent or enemy

syndicate (SIN-di-kit)--a group of gangsters controlling organized crime

tended (TEN-did)--took care of someone or something in a caring way

underling (UHN-dur-ling)--a grunt, or a subordinate who isn't very important

vendetta (ven-DET-uh)--a long-lasting, bitter feud between two parties

BATMAN GLOSSARY

Alfred Pennyworth: Bruce Wayne's loyal butler. He knows Bruce Wayne's secret identity and helps the Dark Knight solve crimes in Gotham City.

Batgirl: Barbara Gordon, a.k.a. Batgirl, is one of Batman's most trusted partners.

Black Mask: also known as Roman Sionis, Black Mask is a ruthless businessman and criminal boss of the Gotham underworld.

False Face Society: an organization of masked criminals who work for Black Mask.

Matches Malone: a two-bit gangster Batman poses as to infiltrate criminal organizations.

Phantasm: despite posing as a man, Phantasm is actually Andrea Beaumont, a deadly martial artist who wields her scythe with expert skill.

The Red Hood: a mysterious villain with a vendetta against Batman. His "hood" is actually a high-tech helmet with a built-in computer.

Utility Belt: each member of the Batfamily owns a Utility Belt that suits their specific crimefighting needs. Each belt contains several compartments with many gadgets that are useful in fighting crime.

VISUAL QUESTIONS & PROMPTS

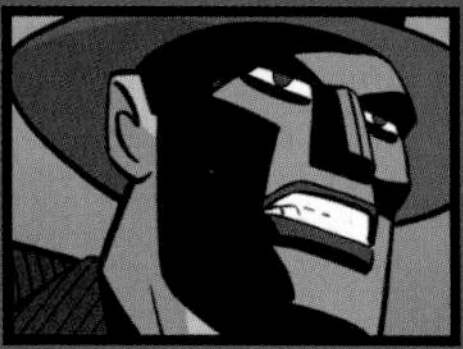

1. Why does Dr. Leslie kiss Alfred on page 6?

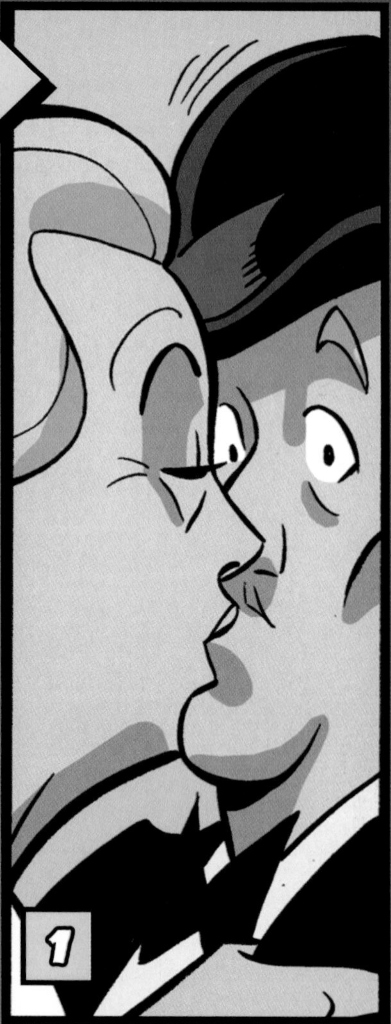
1

2. Several characters in this book wear masks or disguises. What do you think the story has to say about the characters and why they wear the masks or disguises that they do?

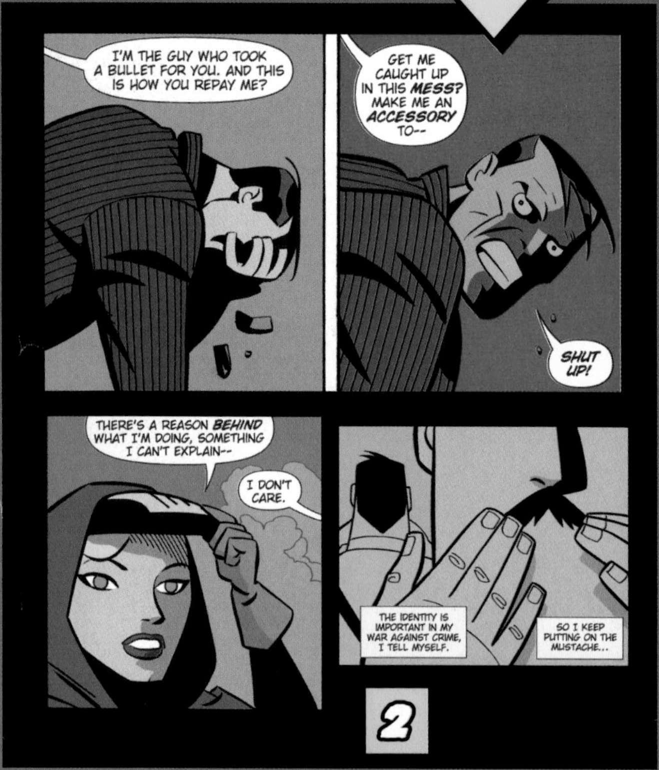
I'M THE GUY WHO TOOK A BULLET FOR YOU. AND THIS IS HOW YOU REPAY ME?
GET ME CAUGHT UP IN THIS MESS? MAKE ME AN ACCESSORY TO--
SHUT UP!
THERE'S A REASON BEHIND WHAT I'M DOING, SOMETHING I CAN'T EXPLAIN--
I DON'T CARE.
THE IDENTITY IS IMPORTANT IN MY WAR AGAINST CRIME, I TELL MYSELF.
SO I KEEP PUTTING ON THE MUSTACHE...
2

3. Read the last two pages of this book again. Describe how Bruce feels about his father in your own words.

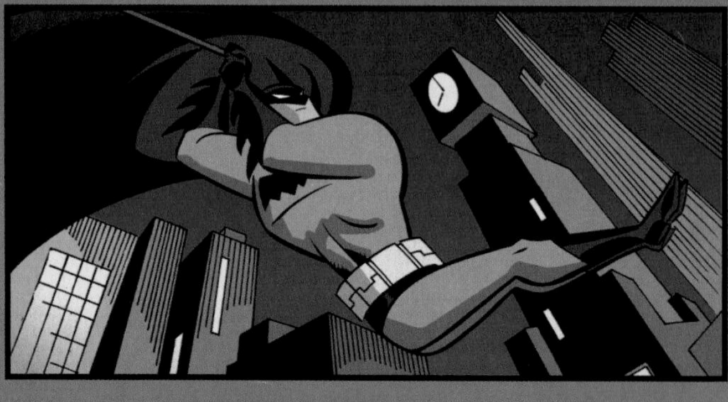

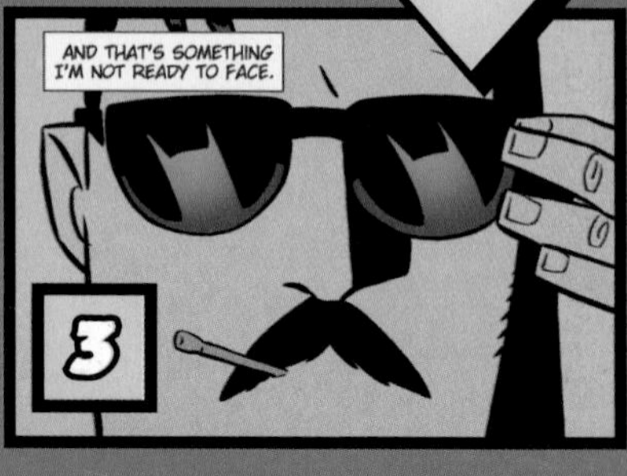
AND THAT'S SOMETHING I'M NOT READY TO FACE.
3

4. Why did Batman choose to use Matches Malone's identity as his disguise? Read page 25 again if you need clues.

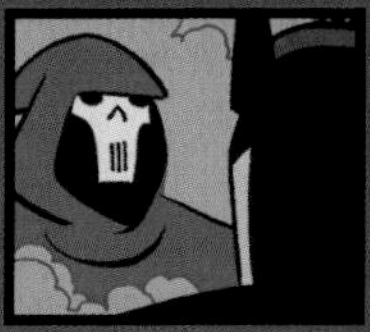

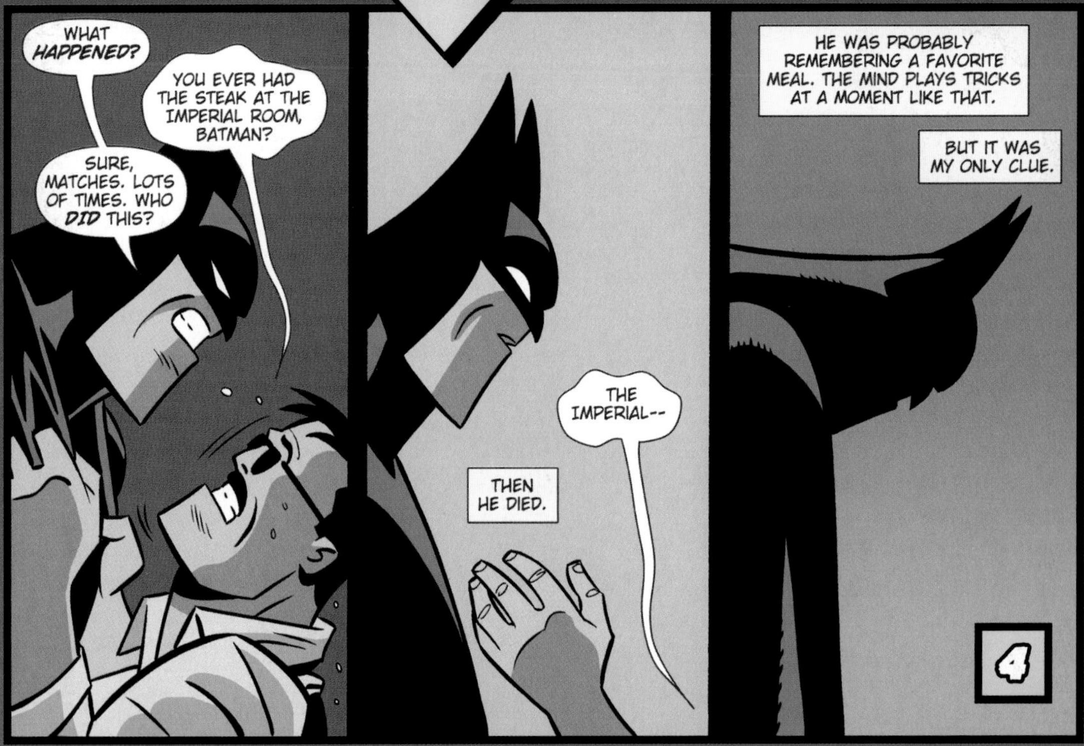
WHAT *HAPPENED?*
YOU EVER HAD THE STEAK AT THE IMPERIAL ROOM, BATMAN?
SURE, MATCHES. LOTS OF TIMES. WHO *DID* THIS?
THE IMPERIAL--
THEN HE DIED.
HE WAS PROBABLY REMEMBERING A FAVORITE MEAL. THE MIND PLAYS TRICKS AT A MOMENT LIKE THAT.
BUT IT WAS MY ONLY CLUE.
4

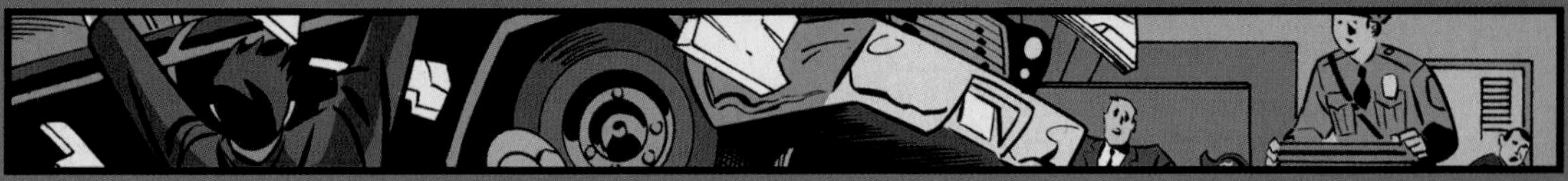

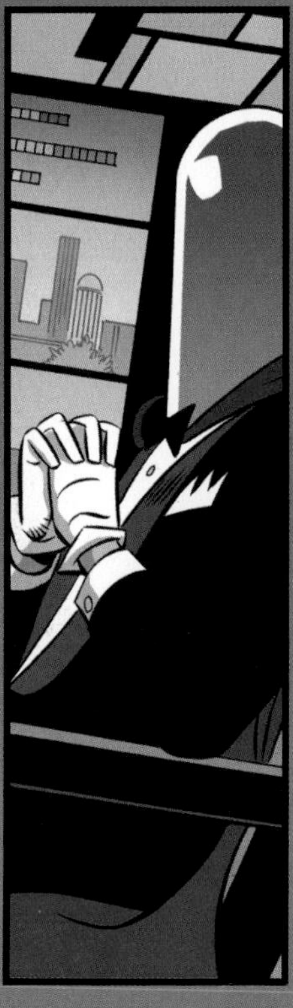

5. Why does Alfred give Dr. Leslie the guardian angel pin? Read the first few pages of this book again if you need clues.

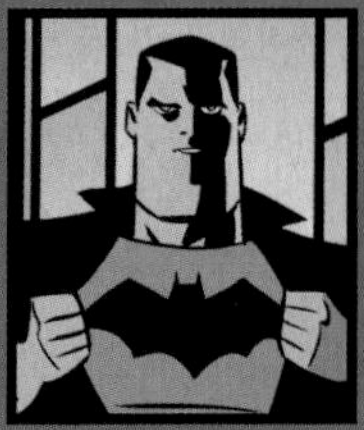

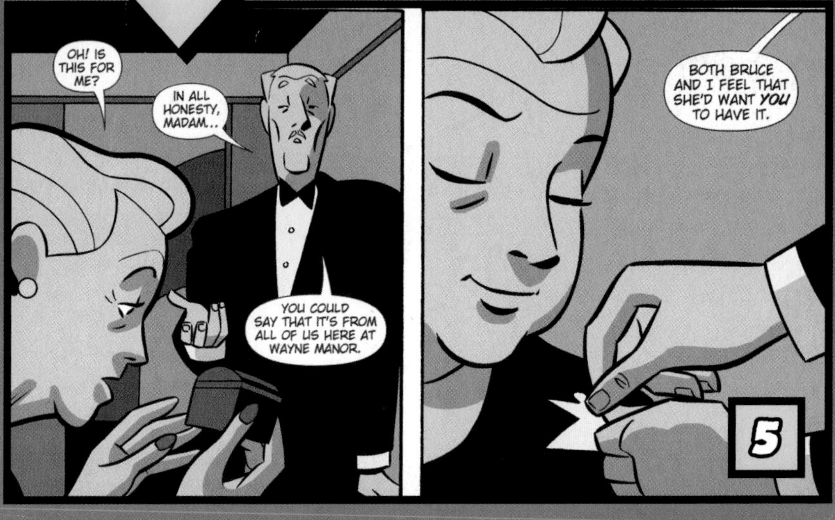
OH! IS THIS FOR ME?
IN ALL HONESTY, MADAM...
YOU COULD SAY THAT IT'S FROM ALL OF US HERE AT WAYNE MANOR.
BOTH BRUCE AND I FEEL THAT SHE'D WANT *YOU* TO HAVE IT.
5